I can see you being invisible

© 2003 Andy Brown
Edited by Robert Allen for NEW WRITERS SERIES

Design by conundrum
Drawings by Andy Brown
Back cover photo by Carrin Christie
Author photo by Monique Dykstra

First Edition
Printed in Canada on 100% recycled paper

National Library of Canada Cataloguing in Publication

Brown, Andy, 1968-
    I can see you being invisible / by Andy Brown.

ISBN 0-919688-85-3 (bound).——ISBN 0-919688-83-7 (pbk.)

    I. Title.

PS8553.R68483I33 2003   C813'.54   C2003-906665-7

DC Books gratefully acknowledges the support of The Canada
Council for the Arts and of SODEC for our publishing program.

Canada Council   Conseil des Arts
for the Arts   du Canada

SODEC
Québec

DC BOOKS / LIVRES DC
C.P. 662, 950 rue Decarie, Montreal, Quebec, H4L 4V9, Canada
www.dcbooks.ca

I can see you being invisible

stories by Andy Brown

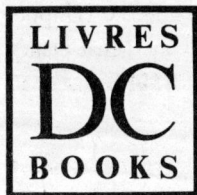

LIVRES DC BOOKS

Tales of Anosmia

Looking for Parking

They worked together in a small publishing firm known for its How-To books. Isaak was currently writing about sheds. She came to his desk and asked if he would accompany her to check on her car. She wanted Isaak's opinion on whether or not she would have to move it, whether she would get a ticket. Isaak was in the middle of a caption on laying rebar for a foundation. The codes for these things were a bitch and he was trying to be generic. He was always trying to be generic.

They put their coats on and went through the lobby of the office. She squealed and went up to the receptionist. Someone had bought a beautiful bouquet of flowers and they were displayed in a vase on the coffee table. She wanted Isaak to smell them and he did. He neglected to tell her that he was anosmiatic and could therefore detect no scent. The flowers were from one of the French programmers who worked all day in the basement.

"There so beautiful. So, so... Spring. Don't you think so, Isaak?"

"Definitely."

"The French are so passionate," she said, glowing.

"There are two sides to passion," he said.

She didn't understand. She often had trouble understanding what he was talking about. "I'll take passion any day. Everything else is so boring," she said.

The sun was out but it was still cold. There was a residual winter wind. The clocks had just sprung forward that weekend. They walked through the rubbled streets of the Old Port, boarded windows and brick. He pointed to the graffiti on a particularly empty brick warehouse which read, "Englishit Go Home". It made her angry.

Then her faced changed and she held her stomach. She had just finished eating her lunch and claimed to have a stomach ache. He sympathized but knew it was the result of her mother's spicy Greek cooking. Isaak would gladly suffer the pain from a tasty home cooked meal. It was strange to him that she still lived with her mother in an all-Greek neighbourhood. He had not been to his parents' home for ten years, except at Christmas.

"Do you think I'll have a ticket?"

"I have no idea." He was growing accustomed to her flipping around conversations like a fish struggling in the bottom of a boat. Her arms kept flailing out to him but he was unsure whether he should take her hand or if she was playfully punching him. When she got like this there was not much he could say. He was simply relieved that she had broken out of her gloom of the week before.

She had called him to come over and he had. They kissed over her mother's laundry machine and he ran his hands over the fabric of her sweater. She had been crying and he wanted to treat her well, because she claimed that no other man ever had.

As they walked the streets of the Old Port Isaak stared at her profile. Her black forest hair curled around her ear. He wanted her to turn and look at him with the depth of her brown eyes. She complained to him often that everyone at the office had blue eyes. He told her that she was lucky to be different. She didn't want to be different.

They passed a semi backing up. A new building was under construction and two men were cutting into concrete with a gigantic saw. She got excited when she saw her car taking up the greater portion of the corner of the next block. It was her mother's boat. She punched him in the stomach playfully and broke into a run. He continued at his pace, observing her enthusiasm. He didn't even have access to a car. Politically, he was opposed to them. He observed an old stone building across a vacant lot. From this perspective it seemed to have been built at a strange angle. It was the only building in the area that did not have boards on the windows. He suddenly remembered the time, ten years before, when he had first arrived in Montreal. He had been broke, living in a rooming house on a street famous for its drug dealers. He had a job punching metal at a factory in this area. Just over there.

She was yelling at him to hurry. The car was a few feet from the curb. It was questionable. "There's no ticket. Do you think I'm okay here? What should I do?"

Isaak found that women were always asking him what they should do.

"If I tell you it's okay and you get a ticket then you'll blame me. It's not like there's a fire hydrant around."

"Let's look for another spot. Come walk with me. You can stand in it until I get the car."

He imagined himself standing between cars in a vacant space, his hands in his pockets, silently waiting for her. The image struck him as ridiculous. They turned around and continued walking, looking for parking. He hoped they would find none.

Sleeves Sewn Shut

I drove the school bus even though I was only thirteen. My father was the town's mechanic, so everyone assumed I knew what I was doing. Some of the kids I drove to the rural high school were older than me. I sat on a thick copy of *Fishes of the World* to see over the yellow hood. At home I kept a notebook where I copied out the lines of fins, scales and eyeballs. My mother had little need for clocks that were not inherited. The only thing she desired was to live in the city, but my father had lied to her before they had been married. It wasn't until after the ceremony that she discovered he had no intention of being more than a mechanic in a small town. Instead they moved in above the garage and had me.

My father would sometimes take me hunting in the afternoons. Mostly for ducks. He wouldn't kill anything he was unwilling to eat, and without refrigeration killing moose or deer seemed excessive.

My father was walking ahead, his eyes searching the long grass. There were rifles suspended under our arms. The metal of the rifle rubbed against my armpit like a coin in a pocket. My father was obsessing over the ghosts hiding in the shadows of the grass. Sometimes a duck burst forth and pulled towards the sky before he lifted the rifle to his shoulder. He still had his hair and it was forever getting in his eyes. He blew a loose strand from his face and took aim. He raised the gun to his eye and the grass bent with a slight shock. The duck shuddered in mid-air, a piece of meat erupting from its side.

My father lowered the rifle and yellow-teethed me. The duck a woman's abandoned glove.

"Fine shot, Pa."

"Gotta always keep your eye ready."

He had worked on hundreds of cars before, but it was not until after the accident that he came to understand their engines: his concentration over gears, the viscosity between his fingers, the intricate scents of gasoline. He kept a pencil behind his ear, and when he went to write out a receipt he would always leave an oily black smudge there.

I had seen my father kill before. Sometimes I would lie down in the grass, disappear, and watch my father retrieve his kill and hold it over his shoulder. As evidence, not glory. He wanted me to be a witness, but I would be hiding in the dry grass, which was stiff and sharp like paper. Driving the school bus had given me a sense of independence. I was beginning to understand roads and where they could take you.

That morning my father didn't come looking. He continued to scour the fields. When he came to a fence he leaned his rifle on the other side, grabbed the wooden railing, and pulled himself over.

It was then I heard it.

I stood up, emerging from the moment as if stepping out of a photograph. The blade of grass fell from my mouth as I ran.

My father was clutching the end of his arm, his hand the accumulation of those lost pieces of meat flying out of ducks. His arm hung from his body like a comma on a blank page. His face was rigid and calm. He was on a boat in the middle of Beaver Lake, falling asleep, watching his fishing line cut into the water. He was in a state of shock.

Pieces of his hand hid under the slivers of the fence. The rifle was still warm when I picked it up. I don't understand why I felt inclined to pick up the fallen rifle and lean it against the fence before I said anything.

"Pa! Oh my God, Pa!"

"I should'a known better."

"We have to do something."

"Give me your shirt."

I gave him my shirt and with surprising strength, considering the circumstances, he ripped off a sleeve with his teeth. He wrapped it around the end of his arm. It was disturbing how calm he was.

"Pull this tight."

I quickly put my torn shirt back on, fumbling with the buttons, conscious of my naked arm. I cradled both rifles under it as we made our way back across the field. The two guns were dancing just above the tips of the grass. My father's face was filled with lines, as if his pain had been drawn on him. I wanted to hold his hand for comfort, but there was an absence at the end of his arm as we ran, staggering with the weight of accident.

I drove the school bus into Napanee, the closest town with a hospital. My father lay on the back seat of the bus, moaning. Every time the bus hit a bump his entire body would be suspended above the seat. In the rear view mirror he looked like a helpless volunteer from the audience being levitated by a magician.

Because I was driving so fast and was unfamiliar with speed at that age, I almost lost control of the bus when it hit a pothole. There was a loud noise before the bus began to lose power. My father yelled from the back to pull over.

At the side of the road I opened the hood for him. Birds left the earth around us. My father reached into the engine with his only hand. A piece of bloody cloth dangled from his other arm, which he held over his head. I could make out a cuff stitched into the cloth. My father maneuvered and twisted his arm through the engine like a question mark. The ends of his hair drooped over his eye, dipping into ink. He was writing that engine.

"Maybe you should put another bandage on. That one's pretty red."

"In a minute." He was breathing hard.

He finished with the engine and pulled his hand out gingerly. I drove the bus the rest of the way to the hospital.

When my mother found out she assumed we would finally move to the city. Instead we stayed above the garage and my father became notorious as the only one-handed mechanic in the province. People would bring their Packards from miles around. She sewed shut the left sleeve on all of his shirts. The black smudges remained above his ear longer before eventually being wiped off.

It was a difficult pregnancy but it took her mind off her grief at losing George. She threw up every morning, felt sick all day. Bucky did all he could to help but there was no reprieve until the baby came. Then it was a different set of problems.

Born without a right arm, little Bucky Jr. got off to the wrong start. As a child he became obsessed with a one-armed baseball player named Pete Gray, who was active during WW II when the league was desperate for players. Gray hit for a .218 average in 234 at bats in his only year in the Bigs, 1945. That was the year the league outlawed dwarfs.

Little Bucky Jr. tried to lead a normal life, and for the most part he was successful. He got along with the other kids; the boys respected his athletic prowess, and soon forgot, in the way boys do, about his handicap. Meanwhile Pete Gray was occupying Bucky Jr.'s mind. He talked about him so much his mother worried this man might only be an imaginary friend. She briefly considered a psychologist, but only went as far as opening the Yellow Pages. Bucky Jr. made his family take their vacation in St. Louis, because Gray had played for the St. Louis Browns. His parents didn't know how to deny him anything. He was an only child.

In St. Louis the family stayed in a Motel 6 by the highway. They saw a baseball game the day after they arrived. The Browns had moved to Baltimore and become the Orioles, but the Cardinals were still there. At the merchandise table Bucky Jr. wanted to know where all the Pete Gray memorabilia was. "Who?" the girl behind the counter said. No cards, no signed photos, no Gray uniform with his number 34 emblazoned on it. Little Bucky Jr. would have given anything to own a Pete Gray glove. In the outfield Gray used to catch the ball with his glove, flip it into the air, tuck his glove under his stump, and catch the ball in his bare hand while he was in the motion of throwing. Bucky Jr. had slowed down the grainy black and white archival videotape over and over until his mother accidentally taped

Mystery over it. His mother wanted desperately for her son to be happy. At least the Cardinals won the game. That was some solace.

Back at the Motel 6 she bought him a Coke. She found it too sweet but her son loved it. Bucky Jr. took the Motel 6 ice bucket and went to get ice. He couldn't find the ice machine however, and wandered the musty yellowing corridor, which smelled of tobacco. A woman came out of one of the rooms. She was young, but all women were old to Bucky Jr. She wore a bathrobe and her blond stringy hair was pushed into an odd shape. Bed head. Her fingernails were bright blue and cracked. Bucky Jr. noted that she'd come out of room 34. He asked her if she knew where the ice machine was. He held up the bucket with his only hand. When she saw the stump at the end of his other arm she was startled but quickly regained her composure, however bleary. "End of the hall, dear," she said smiling.

Emboldened by her friendliness he decided to ask another question. "Is there a Pete Gray memorial around these parts?"

"Who?"

"Never mind."

Bucky Jr. filled the bucket with ice. Holding it by the handle he swung it over his head in a big loop, his arm outstretched. A single ice cube fell to the carpet, left to melt later into a fresh cigarette burn. Back in the room Bucky Jr. was inconsolable. How could no one know who Pete Gray was? If they didn't know him in St. Louis, then where? His father looked at him with his intense blue eyes and told him he should enjoy the vacation. They were a family. Although in the back of his mind he knew they never should have come. How could he explain the passage of time to his son, the limitations of memory? How could he explain that Pete Gray was considered a sideshow in his day? Something to distract the troops.

Back home, Bucky Jr. started a letter-writing campaign to the mayor of St. Louis and to the good people of Nanticoke, Pennsylvania, Gray's home town, asking if they would please consider a memorial. The secretary for the St. Louis mayor responded to the first few letters saying it was under consideration but she was doubtful, and eventually she stopped responding at all. Bucky Jr. founded a web page devoted to Gray. He discovered that Gray had played for Trois Rivières in the Minors and actually hit a home run once. He made a poorly designed zine, cutting and pasting statistics and the few photos he could find. Scissors were sometimes difficult.

His mother was worried about his obsession, but was somewhat consoled by the fact that he was being so creative. She couldn't imagine who he could have got it from. Bucky couldn't draw a line and she only read *Reader's Digest*. She thought of George and his amazing watercolours. She remembered a flattering portrait he had painted of her once, before it all happened. For some reason George had painted her eyes brown like his own, when hers were blue. She hadn't thought of him since becoming pregnant. And she knew Bucky wanted to forget. He hadn't even gone to the funeral.

Soon Bucky Jr. forgot all about Pete Gray and, after a brief flirtation with Jim Abbott, the one-handed pitcher who hurled a no-hitter for the Yankees in 1993, he wanted to be a scientist. His parents were relieved. It wasn't until the grade nine science teacher taught basic Mendelian genetics that Bucky Jr. figured it out. He argued with the teacher, telling him this Mendel person must have it all wrong. The teacher was adamant but sympathetic. It happened once every few years when he told the class about the gene for eye colour, and how, because of dominant and recessive genes it is impossible for two blue-eyed parents to have a brown-eyed child.

The Sacrifice

Again we go for coffee at a very French café, with her looking like Zelda before the memoirs. Back in the days of being Daisy, wearing leather jackets and sunglasses everywhere. She is a Russian ballerina who practices voodoo. We hold hands at the table while she tells me of a jealous lover and how she might be deported back to the States. She needs to get married. She tried to explain to Immigration that she is a skate-boarder from the Big A, but no one at Immigration can speak English.

Out of the window we watch as a man wearing a white coat covered in blood unloads a truck. A sheep drapes over his shoulder, the tongue dangling. It is slit from the throat to the penis, its full, thick wool now bloody. She playfully shades my eyes for me. Vegetarian nightmare. The man carries the sheep into the front door of a shop. He has trouble opening the door for the dead animal. She lets me into her world over a *café-au-lait*. I step over the line between us only to find the snow quickly cover it up. The next time it is a piglet draped over his shoulder. It is lightly snowing and the flakes turn to water on the window. I notice ribs. Not much meat on the beast as it makes its way through the cold and into the comfort of the freezer. The man in the blood-stained coat finishes his delivery. He will stop on the way home to buy cigarettes. The store owner, suspicious of blood, will call the cops, thinking the man has just committed a heinous crime.

A reptilian Zelda caresses my hand and tells me she has stopped taking elevators. She tells me of her pain. Later we climb the stairs to her loft. A fanged idol with a toy ray gun guards her bed. In the morning I wake up to discover that I have been slit from my throat to my penis. I notice ribs. I hear the fetal sound of traffic. She wakes up and puts on her panties. She stares out the window, watching the traffic below. I lie there losing blood, unable to move. She picks up the telephone and dials. She tells the person on the other end that she has another one for them to pick up. Time passes uncertainly before a man in a fresh white coat comes in to drape me over his shoulder as if he were burping a helpless child.

Caleb's Auto

It was while racing through fields of sunflowers which all faced the same direction that Isaak noticed the red oil light flashing on the Volkswagen dashboard. The smoke billowing out of the engine faded into the distance of the landscape. The sky became thick with blue cloud. A cyclist passed in the opposite direction, holding his hand over his mouth. The oil light was frantic.

Isaak made it to a deserted tourist stop. Autumn had come to the lake; there were orange and brown leaves floating at the water's edge.

A chip stand and a gas station were the only buildings around. He pulled up to the pumps and asked the elderly mechanic for eight litres of 10W30 oil. Isaak needed so much oil because it was pouring out of the engine like a slit throat.

"Maybe you shouldn't be driving that," the mechanic said slowly.

"It'll be all right. I just need eight litres to get me to the Volkswagen dealership in Kingston. Maybe I can sell her for parts."

"Yeah. Parts.... Just a minute."

He disappeared into the wooden building. There was a plate glass window with a red insignia — Caleb's Auto. Grease had started to claim the lower corners of the window, turning them nearly opaque. He came out.

"You must be Caleb."

"Yeah. How did you know? Were you around the lake this year?"

"Your window."

He turned and looked at the building, the place with his name, as if for the first time. He lifted his grimy baseball cap with his only hand and tucked it under his opposite armpit where the sleeve of his shirt had been sewn shut. He ran his hand through his hair, leaving a trace of grease. He looked at Isaak.

"You can't go."

"What do you mean?"

"I only got two litres of oil. Never make it."

Isaak thanked Caleb and went to the chip stand. It was a white trailer firmly fixed onto a worn patch of ground. Beyond it was a length of grass, just wide enough to get a kite up, and then the lake. The water looked cold and the playground was empty. Isaak knocked on the glass of the trailer as he read the sign on which the various sizes of fries were listed. It felt inevitable that he would order the medium. Because he liked to avoid extremes Isaak never ordered the large or small; he always tried to see both sides, stay uncommitted. The clouds were being reflected by the lake.

"Hello, can I help you?" said the chip girl, startling him.

"One medium please."

She disappeared into the back of the trailer again. Isaak looked across the road, to where the car was cooling, and saw Caleb looking back at him from behind his window. The chip girl returned with the medium fries.

"Is there another gas station around here?" Isaak asked as she gave him more ketchup packs.

"Well there's Caleb there. Hey Bets," she yelled into the back of the trailer, "You know any other gas stations around here?"

"Don't know of one," came a voice from the back.

"Sorry."

Isaak sat on a picnic bench, exposed to the raw wind off the lake. It carried the scent of detritus and water. It knocked down dragon flies and whipped images out of his mind. Suddenly Isaak felt as if he were being watched.

He turned to see Caleb walking toward him. The old man was saying something but he was talking into his shoes and the wind intercepted his voice.

"What?"

"I said I'd like to give ya fifty bucks for the car."

"Thanks but I'm sure I can do better at the dealership."

Then, thinking he might have hurt his feelings, Isaak quickly added, "It's a piece of shit, you wouldn't want it."

"Maybe I got some others like it somewhere."

"Do you? You mean you collect 411s?

"Well… no." But he wouldn't say anything more. He turned and walked back into his building. The one with the name he had already forgotten.

When Isaak finished his fries he went into Caleb's Auto and found him standing on a chair screwing in a light bulb with his only hand. When he had finished Isaak asked him for his two litres.

"It won't get ya far enough. Of that I'm sure."

"Well. We'll see. And do you have any Coke?"

"Ya. In back. Just a sec."

He left Isaak with the two litres he had taken from under the counter and disappeared into the back. It was then that Isaak leaned over the counter, his belt buckle digging into his stomach, and discovered a whole row of oil bottles under there, their plastic seals unbroken. When Caleb came back with the Coke, Isaak paid him.

"How bout a hunerd?"

"I think I'll just try to make it to Kingston, thanks."

"Sure. Just thought I could help."

Isaak went out the door into the lot and put the two litres of oil in the car. All or nothing. No more mediums. Later, as the smoke turned blue, he started to wonder about what it was that inhabited Caleb's sky, and how long it could stay aloft.

I can see you being invisible

He's still there when I wake up. I look out my third floor window, which faces the street, and see him sitting with his arms crossed on the same bench as yesterday. Every morning I check out the window and every morning he's either on that bench, the one in front of the depanneur, or the one across from the bank. He hasn't moved more than a block in four days.

He wears a red sweatshirt and dirty white pants. His black hair covers the back of his neck. He's thin, with a beard growing out of control, like a homeless Christmas elf. He doesn't ask for money, he barely moves his head. Perhaps he was let out of a sanitarium and once lived in the area, but upon returning was confused by the Starbucks on the corner, the mini-skirts with cellphones relaxing on crowded terraces. He can only recognize asphalt, benches, and the scars left by ancient streetcars.

It's as if he's waiting for someone. Waiting for the girl who never came, waiting for his dealer. Watching him, I am reminded of my youth in Vancouver and the ubiquitous freighters looming in the harbour, waiting offshore for months. His presence on the bench is like a dream I can't quite remember but which stays with me all day.

I keep returning to my window throughout the day, checking to see if he's gone. I do the laundry and he's there on his bench, I watch *The Simpsons*, cook dinner, still he's there, scratching his head intermittently. Every time I go to the window he's there. Sometimes I notice he's not on his regular bench, but when I leave the house and walk down the street I see him sitting one block away on a different bench. He doesn't lie down and sleep, he just sits. Legs straight out, toes pointing up. People pass him on their way to work, then again when they come home, their arms loaded down with groceries. It's the fact that he does nothing wrong that makes him so disturbing. He doesn't beg or shout, or lie around comatose. He just sits. His endurance is unnerving. Of what is he capable?

On the seventh day he is still there. Then again on the eighth. If only he would keel over and pass out so that someone could call an ambulance. If only he would attack someone so that the police could be summoned. But he just sits, waiting, arms crossed, as if to accuse, oblivious to any expectations. Being ignored to death.

I spend my days doing research for a film company which is making a documentary about the revitalization of the public pools around Montreal. The pools were built by the city during the Depression because very few of the apartments on the Plateau had running water. At the time the area was filled with Jewish refugees. Now that the neighbourhood is being gentrified, the Toronto dotcoms moving into condos, these public pools are being demolished or renovated. The film company also moved here from Toronto, to take advantage of the cheap rents, but working for them is better than welfare. I spend my days interviewing lifeguards, plumbers, and architects, checking the neighbourhood for clues.

I was initially interested in working for the film company because I've been swimming for years at the Piscine Shubert. Before it was renovated there was a single shower room, which made the pool unisex. Little old men came in and spent half an hour in the shower, scrubbing their hunched liver-spotted bodies. There were six-foot-tall porcelain urinals along one wall, like upright canoes. Now there are lockers and tiny shower stalls, wheelchair access, and shoe box urinals.

The dep on the corner is run by a large Greek family and sells Bouzouki CDs. Most of their business comes from the post office they run from the back. When I go in to buy a Diet Coke I ask one of the family's many sons if he knows who the stranger is.

"I have no idea. He just showed up."

"So, you've noticed him sitting out there."

"Yeah. The security guard at the bank said to be careful."

"Well... the security guard is paid to be paranoid. Besides

the guy sits directly across from the bank all day."

"Still, I'm gonna be careful."

That night, when I return home late from interviewing retired lifeguards, he is pacing the sidewalk in front of my building. His swaying gait is more tired than drunk. I avoid eye contact, pull out my keys, and bound up my stairs. As I unlock the door I turn to look at him moving slowly down the street. His red sweatshirt is now baggy and hanging off him. I have some left-over chili in a yogurt container in my fridge. I consider bringing this out to him. What harm could it do? But to do so would make me responsible. He watches me every day, knows where I live. His is an act of public starvation.

I run into my neighbour on the street and he asks me if I've noticed the stranger who has "moved in." My neighbour is worried that the man has come up from New York for retribution. He tells me about living in the Bronx and working for some shady businessmen. They bought a truck under my neighbour's name because they didn't want to use their names on the insurance. He did deliveries for them and didn't ask questions. When he found a dead body on his couch one morning he took the truck and made a run for the border. He used it for a couple of summers in Montreal, to do freelance moving before the insurance ran out. Our landlady is now threatening to take him to the *Régie*; she wants to renovate. I fear I might not have many years left in this building myself. I find it amazing that he would think the stranger on the bench is in the mob, but then I realize that this man, sentinel and patient, is becoming a physical manifestation of our guilty secrets, our past crimes. We read into his presence what we want to forget.

On day thirteen it rains. From the window I check for him in his usual spots, but he's gone. Off to find shelter, or perhaps he has a home. He must have eaten in thirteen days. Twice I witnessed him drinking from a clear bottle what appeared to be either mineral water or club soda. Once I saw him smoke. The rain is light at first, but soon becomes a torrent. I'm thankful he's not out there on a bench getting soaked.

I have an appointment at the library archives, so I need to leave the house in this weather. I take an umbrella which, when clumsily folded, is shaped like a bat. Descending to the street I catch him out of the corner of my eye. He's standing under a doorway, two doors down from me, shifting from foot to foot. I unfurl the bat umbrella and quickly fly down the street, eager to get to the underground safety of the Metro. I'm late for the appointment and miss out on the tour of the cryogenically preserved tomes in the basement. When I return home he is still there, in the doorway. I realize that I don't even know who lives at that address anymore.

That night I dream of all my darkest secrets. The time I shat my pants on the grade five field trip, petty thefts, betrayal.

On day seventeen I witness a fight at the bagel shop. The underpaid Bangladeshis need to be separated, fists flailing, too close to the oven. They scream in a language none of us in line can understand. I yell at them to stop from behind the counter, conscious of the knives in the room, but they ignore me. On the way home I spot him hovering outside my building. I hold the brown paper bag filled with sesame bagels to my chest, keeping me warm. I leave a piping hot bagel on the bench outside the dep. The next day it is gone.

Finally I make eye contact. What looked like freckles from a distance reveal themselves to be flakes of dirt. Little brown details. His clothes are filthy as well, his nose twisted, his beard almost a mask. When he looks at me it seems, just for a flash, that there is some hint of recognition in his eyes.

When I notice *Coast Guard* listed in the telephone book next to *Community Pools* I think of Spence. Of course. The stranger on the bench is Spence. Or could be. The nose is what gives it away. It's hard to tell but he's about the right age.

Jimmy Spencer's father drove the hovercraft for the Vancouver Coast Guard. I became friends with Spence when his father took the two of us out for a ride on the wetlands surrounding the airport. When the engine started and the skirt of the hovercraft filled with air I couldn't contain my excitement. The hovercraft skated over the sand dunes, the water, the surface of things. I was amazed by its speed. I had to close my eyes when Spence's father didn't even slow down as the craft hit land. Nothing could stop us.

Spence was a sickly kid with jet black hair and a distinctive nose like a broken umbrella. He still had the trace of a British accent, which lingered even though his family had emigrated many years before. My mother told me that I always befriended the boy no one else liked.

Spence and I used to play street hockey in the drained wading pool in the park because neither of us could skate. We would play with whatever boys happened to be around. I had these blue plastic shin guards which we used as goalie pads. During one game I checked Spence a little too aggressively and his legs buckled over the edge of the wading pool concrete. His nose came down hard. Suddenly blood was spurting everywhere but my only concern was that I had broken my stick. Spence spat at me with the blood running into his mouth. I held a slim piece of wood in my hand, the other end lay motionless in the empty pool, the blade a perfect curve.

After palming the quarters our parents had intended for the collection plate at church Spence and I would walk home past the Korean market. We stood before the candy counter with our quarters gleaming in anticipation.

When my sister described the act to my parents she phrased it as "stealing from the collection plate," but I preferred not to think of myself as a thief. Once the money was in my hand it was mine to do with as I pleased. I couldn't picture the orphans for whom the money was intended. I didn't know any orphans. I simply chose not to donate my money. We bought our candies at the counter where an old Korean woman would smile at us. Often we would buy hockey cards. I would trade to get all the cards with players from the Boston Bruins. This was because Bobby Orr played on the Bruins.

When the quarters progressed to a dollar Spence and I became more daring. We had taken to practicing in front of a mirror. The bills tucked easier into my sleeve than the cumbersome coins. One Sunday after church, I noticed Spence pocket a couple of packs of hockey cards while picking up another two from the box. He proceeded to the counter to pay for the two with his bill, the Korean woman smiling. Outside the store I told him that I'd seen what he'd done. I was unsure whether I should chastise or admire him. In one of his packs was Bobby Orr, flying through the air triumphant, having just scored a goal.

It wasn't long before I was caught. I had forgotten about mirrors. The Korean woman was irate. She had seen everything in the convex mirror in the corner of the ceiling. I never went back to the Korean market and I started to mow lawns for the next door neighbour so that I could have my own money to put in the collection plate every Sunday. Like his father's hovercraft my friendship with Spence skated over water and land with surprising agility. There was no diving into the depths. And now that could be Spence stationed on the bench across the street from my apartment, waiting for me to make a mistake.

He is about the same age, has the same nose, the hockey hair. I grow convinced that he's Spence. I make up lengthy scenarios in my head, projecting a past for him, trying to decipher the circumstances which led him to that bench. His troubled life of crime, his father's disappointment at his mechanical ineptitude. I search for hovercrafts on the Web.

I wait one month before sitting on the bench beside him. He doesn't acknowledge me at all. He leans forward with his arms crossed and inspects his shoes, which are stained blue from something. His beard is scraggly, not a thick block on his face, less a mask than an extension of his weak chin. He could be

Spence. I never knew him when we were old enough to have facial hair, but it definitely could be him. I hadn't planned on whether I would talk to him or not. I only thought it out as far as this moment.

I get up from the bench and go into the dep for a bottle of Diet Coke. I can't help it, I'm addicted. I return to the bench and this time he looks at me. His eyes are a little bloodshot but otherwise quite lucid. He doesn't appear to recognize me. I nod my head at him and sit down. To avoid having to talk I quickly occupy myself with opening the Diet Coke and checking under the cap to see if I'm suddenly rich. *Sorry try again.*

I get up from the bench and go into the dep. Inside, the fluorescent light gives everything a jaundiced glow. The sounds of Bouzouki fill the store. I notice the convex mirrors, strategically placed. I purchase two singles because the son behind the counter knows me. I'm in there all the time and I've never bought a pack.

I return to the bench and he looks at me again. I nod my head and sit down. I offer him one of the cigarettes filter first. The gesture is like a teacher pointing out a distant land on a map. He ignores the cigarette, so I pocket them both. He breathes steadily, looking straight ahead, and I work up my nerve. After the weeks of constant speculation all I am capable of doing is to blurt out, "Spence?"

He turns his head slowly. He has no need for speed. The scraggled mat on his face parts as he says, "*Quoi?*"

His language comes as a shock to me. It's as if the hovercraft hit land and skidded to a halt instead of gliding on.

I stop looking out my window, stop looking for him. The film crew starts production and I am out of the apartment for entire afternoons. He becomes invisible to me until I notice him a few days later showering in the tiny stall at the Piscine Shubert, all wet and gleaming. He is still there after my swim.

How to Build a Wall in 12 Easy Steps

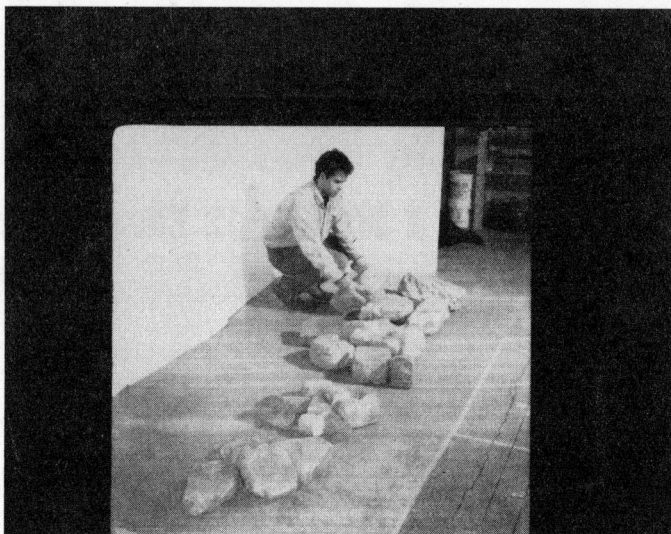

1 I started a new job. It consisted of going to a studio and building sets while she took pictures. I would spend alternate weeks in an office writing the step-by-step instructions for what I had done the week before. Although it sounded like a reasonable enough plan, it soon became an exercise in the theatre of the absurd.

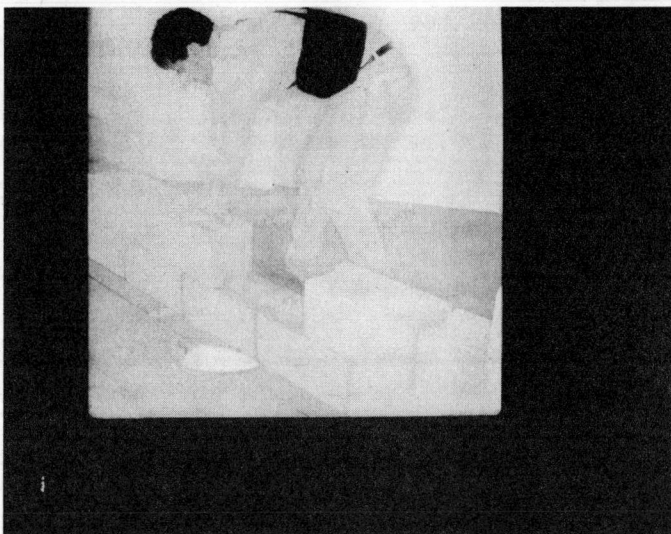

2 The office was in a restored building in the Old Port, the construction of which had won some awards. It was a labyrinthine place, full of staircases and cramped alcoves. There were black and white photographs on the walls in strategic places. They showed the same spot at the time of construction, with its unfinished walls and ancient stone warehouse niches. Looking at the photograph with one eye and the refurbished hallway in front of you with the other was like tricking time.

3 *If you're building a brick or stone wall that will require mortar you need to be confident that it will rest on a solid footing. Any shifting of the ground will create cracks in the wall and may lead to a future tumbling.*

4 Later I would develop a penchant for looking very closely at brick walls, determining their bond patterns, the concentrations of cement. I'd see wythes where others would see rows. I came to view a wall as a history of its construction.

5 He never really talked about anything except his ambivalence towards her. How she was a photographer who was unphotogenic.

6 *Pour the concrete into the forms. Don't knock yourself out leveling and smoothing the concrete with a darby or trowel. Nobody ever sees the footing once the wall is built.*

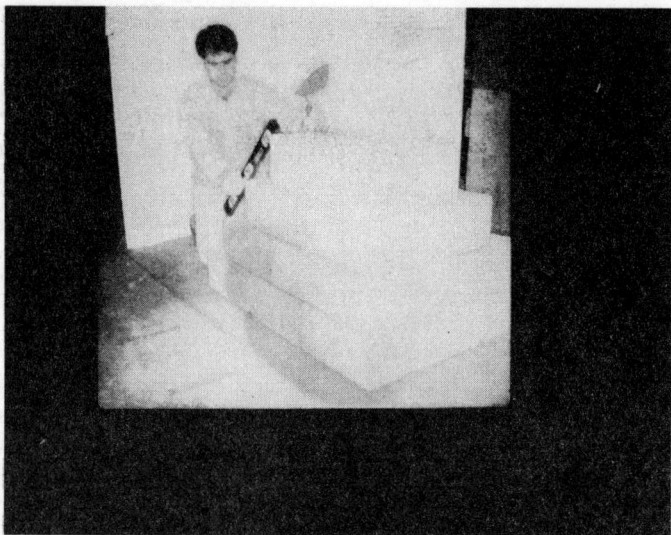

7 Surrounding the lens of her black steel camera was a light tube, the size and shape of a halo, which acted as a flash. I laid out strings and levels and she flashed me with her halo. While the photo developed we chatted idly, or I ran off to phone the consultant, who lived on a mountain in the wilds of California.

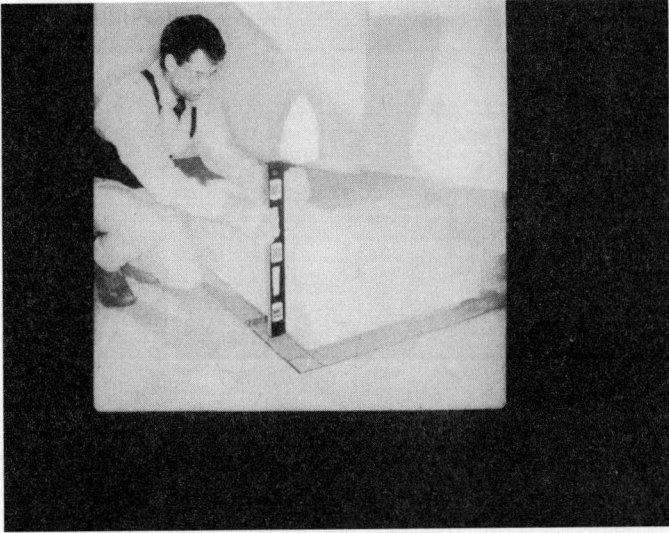

8 I began to build leads in the studio. Build up the corners, the ends of walls. Instead of mortar we used day-glo oatmeal. The idea when building a wall is to start at the ends and work toward the middle. She was not too eager for leads. She wanted anyone who was not him. She wanted to start from the middle and build straight up quickly.

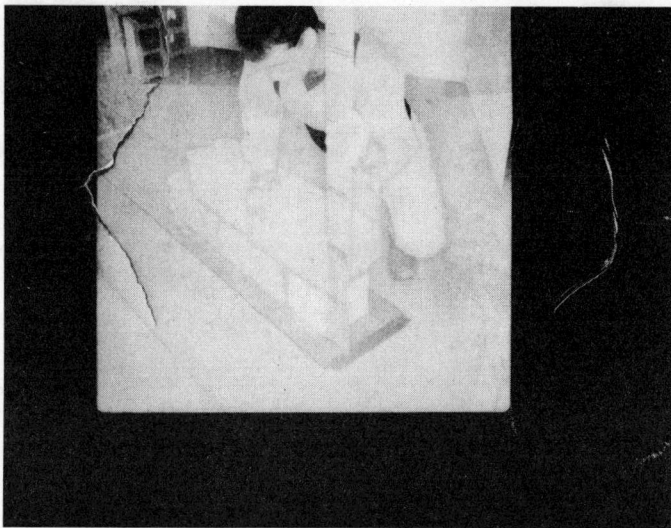

9 *Hold a storeypole vertically against the wall to keep track of the height of the courses. Adjust to fit the story.*

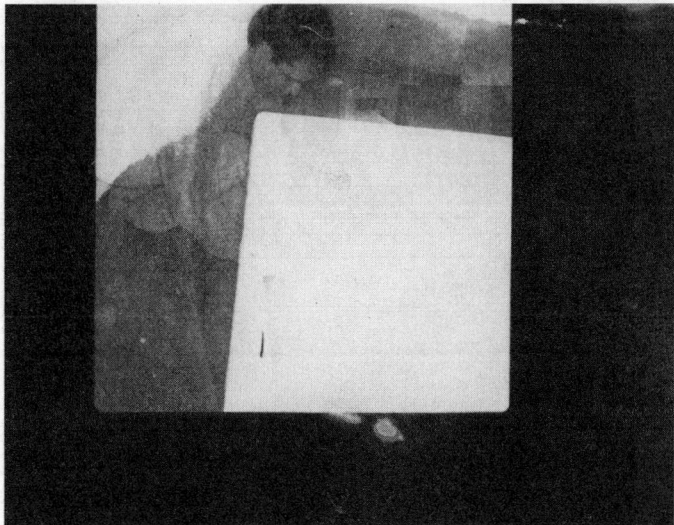

10 In the photograph you can just barely make out his fist following through. Coming from the edge of the frame. I am stumbling back into the trench, a look of mortification on my face. The image is slightly out of focus. The night before he had stayed late at the office and read the history of our e-mail.

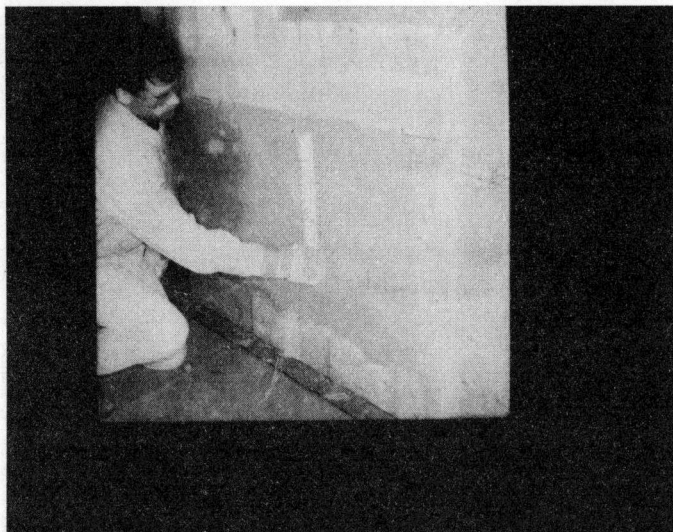

11 *John Devitt has spent the last ten years on the road, living for his portable 252 foot long replica of the Vietnam Memorial in Washington. He travels ten months a year, hitting about 28 cities. He drives a truck attached to a flatbed trailer that carries the Moving Wall. One friend says John is a good correspondent, but has no interest outside the Wall: "I would say this has taken over his life in a pretty serious way."*

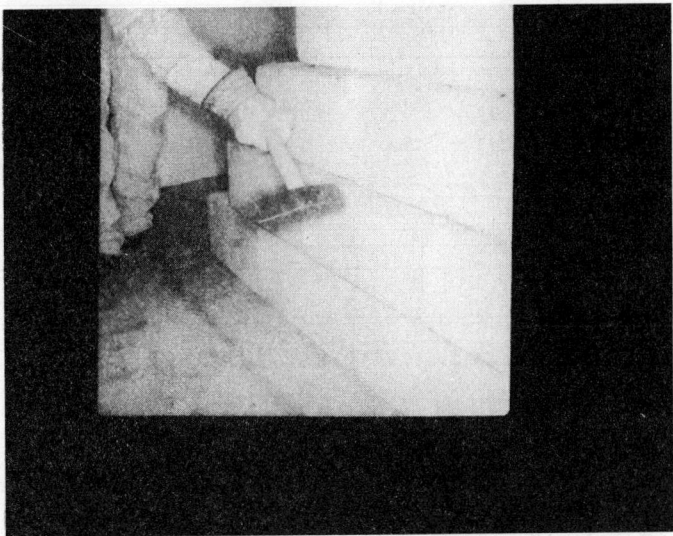

12 Anything can be built on ruins.

Writers Get Real Jobs

Bakhtin on Sabbatical

Isaak searches all over for Uzma that night in his dream. A transvestite plays the piano in the corner of a loft party. It is Isaak and Uzma's loft. Uzma has invited the world and now Isaak can no longer find her. He searches everywhere. Strangers sit on his furniture. Someone is rolling joints in the corner. Isaak searches every face, he searches the carnival for her.

Bakhtin is in a corner discussing wine, wearing a charcoal suit, hands folded on his knee. He is passed a joint and inhales in a practiced way. He stands up and goes to play the piano, pushing the transvestite aside. Words come out instead of notes. Soaking wet, drowned words because the piano was rescued from the sea. Bakhtin conducts his carnival here in the loft before Isaak opens his eyes to the dark.

Bakhtin is becoming tired of his job at the University. He wants perspective, not theory. He is tired of egg salad sandwiches in brown paper bags. He gives his charcoal suit to the Salvation Army and lets his hair grow long and curly. He buys shoes six sizes too large and yellow daisies for his lapel. His nose is thin, too thin for the rubber nose to stay on, so he uses an elastic around his head. He stays up late at night practicing his accordion and watching video tapes of *The Dick Van Dyke Show*. Bakhtin takes a sabbatical from academia to become a clown.

At the mime school Bakhtin is the star. He and his silent wit. He learns all the standards: pulling the rope, in the box and can't get out, heavy object over the head. He impresses the teachers by acting out their dreams for them. He never talks but he carries a notebook around his neck on a string. Clipped to it is a pencil, which sometimes goes behind his ear. No one in the mime school writes in it so it remains blank except for Bakhtin's musings on Reader Response Theory, a book by a man named after a trout. Bakhtin may be a mime but he still reads voraciously.

Bakhtin graduates from the mime school with honours and considers going into real estate. He will never get the white mask off of his face. For Isaak, Uzma no longer beside him, this causes him to mistake Bakhtin for a ghost every night he dreams him.

Booked into the Wartime

William Faulkner was let go from MGM and hadn't written a book in years. He was forced to move into a trailer park and drive a cab. Every morning at five he was on the road, the glove compartment filled with bourbon. The other cabbies told him he should have a gun in there. It was not that William had anything against guns, hell he used to love to shoot his rifle at ducks; no, he just needed the space for the day's nourishment.

He started driving for Mary's Taxi. He made his way to the garage every morning and they gave him a car and gas. He gave Mary sixty percent of the money on the sheet at the end of the night. Not that William would write down all his fares. He neglected to mention the couple needing the lift those few blocks, the guy who puked in the back and William demanding fifty bucks on the spot, the quick fares, the rides.

He usually parked outside the Market in the Wartime. This was the name of the area he was booked into. William assumed it had something to do with the veterans being given houses after the War and the town growing around them. He sat in the parking lot, the glove compartment door a shelf for the bourbon. He was thinking of his General in his head, imagining the Wartime as his Yoknapatawpha County and the Market as his Jackson. He imagined the people as characters in a hamlet: those he brought submarines, the postmen he sometimes took on a route, the young mothers he took out to the penitentiary, the drunk men who came out of basements needing a ride to Club 69 and insisting that William join them for a drink, or the young student at six AM trying out for the rowing team. He imagined where commas would fall in the squawk coming over the radio, the dispatcher's voice terminal. William couldn't write for too long in his head any more, because he needed to concentrate on the dispatcher's voice.

"Fifty-two. Three-forty-four Union. That's a callback, fifty-two. Seventeen. The Checker. Is that you Hank?"

And another voice, "Sure is. You finished tying that number four Mosquito?"

"Gotta get a new kind of thread. Go ahead thirty-one."

"Wartime."

"Needs to be stronger for the deeper inlets. You're number two in the Wartime thirty-one."

The endless thread of voice. William knew he was number one in the Wartime, and he was going to get a call.

"Twenty-six, the Market, south entrance." William was car twenty-six.

"Roger."

Directly ahead of him was the young woman who must have called, because she waved her arms frantically as he approached. He took a swig of Wild Turkey and put the cap back on the bottle. He added it to the one already an object of remorse in the glove compartment. As he put the cab into drive and swung it in to pick up the woman, he turned off the dispatcher's voice.

She had obviously been crying. William Faulkner thought it was rather odd that she had no groceries with her. That was the whole point of parking outside the Market. All the fares had groceries and you could charge extra for it. That was the policy anyway. It was usually older women, sometimes hunched, that he would find here. The students were near the University zone and the business crowd was Downtown, but William preferred it a little out of the way. The Wartime was always the least busy zone.

The young woman entered his cab and told him to drive. She had on a short patterned dress and a hoop in her eyebrow. Her black hair was cropped short, William bet it was with a razor blade. She was trying to hide the fact that she had been crying.

"No groceries?"

"What?"

"No groceries. The supermarket."

"Oh, right. No. It was the closest phone, just drive, please."

"Where?"

"Wherever." William gave her his handkerchief and she laughed at the absurd act of chivalry. She blew her nose and put it in her pocket. "What's your name?"

"Bill."

"I'm Ursula."

"Listen, Ursula. If you don't actually want to go anywhere in particular, as is my assumption…"

"Sorry. Yeah, I guess. It's just my boyfriend…"

"Say no more, Ursula. We shall go to the track, you and I. There's a horse in the seventh that we may just catch."

"Whatever, Bill. Thanks."

"I'm taking you off the meter. But maybe you could put some money down on *Taxidermy Bound* and give me a percentage of your winnings."

"You're kidding, right? *Taxidermy Bound*? What kind of a name is that?"

But William Faulkner said nothing more until they were at the track. After turning off the meter he put some music on the radio. Ursula admitted to liking the band that was playing. William didn't care much for hip-hop.

As soon as they arrived William took a full bottle out of the glove compartment and put it into his pocket. Ursula noticed this with trepidation.

They were just in time for the seventh race. William asked for twenty bucks from Ursula and she gave it to him. He bet this, as well as the fifty he had received earlier from the vomiting passenger, on *Taxidermy Bound*. He then bought a race form and started pointing out to Ursula all the horses from Kentucky.

"I will only bet on a horse if it is from the South," he told her.

She asked him questions about the form, what all the columns and numbers were about, and he explained about mud shoes and the home lives of the jockeys.

"You are quite a gentleman," she told him.

They watched the race from the rail. William took out his bottle and Ursula asked for some. He obliged. *Taxidermy Bound* came up from third. The rumble of the hooves crashed into the soil. William collected at three to one.

With their windfall they were going to celebrate. Ursula confided that she fell in love too easily. William confessed that he had been wanting to ask her why she'd pierced her eyebrow.

"Research," she said. And nothing more was said about it. William was a gentleman after all.

They got back into the taxi and had some more Wild Turkey.

"There's a good rib place out on the old road." William knew the city well.

"I don't eat meat."

William started to drive Downtown instead. They were bound to find something there. He turned on the radio and the dispatcher's voice came out in monotone, seemingly still on the same sentence. William booked off, said he was going to dinner. It struck Ursula that his Southern drawl was becoming more pronounced, that he must be quite drunk. Along Main Street he turned around and asked her whether her hair had been cut with a razor. Before she could answer a silver Jetta smashed into the side of his cab.

When he opened his eyes a few moments later, Ursula was draped across the seat, a bubble of blood over her eye. She was unconscious but breathing calmly. Bourbon was dripping from the broken bottles in the glove compartment, the floor sticky with it. William cupped his hands under the flow of golden liquid and put it to his lips. He then exited the taxi and asked the first person in the crowd forming where he could get a bus to the rib place out on the old road.

It wasn't until he had satiated himself with expensive ribs that William Faulkner remembered leaving number twenty-six abandoned in the heart of the Wartime.

Pawn Shop Suitor

Jane Austen lost all of her privileges and opened up a pawn shop in the east end of the city. Customers would come to her looking for watches, VCRs, televisions. But Jane liked showing everyone the jewelry. It was the jewelry she had owned which enabled her to procure the capital to open the shop. She had a penchant for the soft sell with the jewelry, it was what she knew. But she had no idea how to set the clock on the VCR, let alone how to manoeuvre in the tiny shop with her huge bell of a dress. People came in looking for laptops and she asked them about their love lives. Unless they wanted jewelry, she wasn't much help.

She languished at the pawn shop for months until a man looking for a stopwatch caught her attention. She was coy. He came back the next day looking for a camcorder. She began to wonder if this attractive man wasn't really just coming into the shop to flirt with her. He was remarkably friendly. He asked her about her dress, whether she got terribly sweaty wearing it. He came back the same day for a cell phone. He is obviously interested, thought Jane Austen. Why would anyone need these things?

One week later this man came into the pawn shop again. Jane was bored, polishing some gems, when the tinkle of the bell signaled his arrival. He wanted a gun. Jane sold him a handgun for one hundred dollars.

The next day the man came in again and sold her some jewelry. It was quality merchandise. Jane knew her jewelry and knew she could turn a pretty penny. She smiled at him and playfully twirled her long curled tresses with her thin fingers. Jane Austen was in love, she was sure of it.

Joyce on the Second Storey

Joyce was getting tired of writing on table cloths and decided to take a job with a framing crew. The first impression from the crew boss was that Joyce was a frail little man whose glasses were extremely thick, but there was a desperate need for labourers at that moment.

Joyce just wanted to use his hands for something other than writing. No longer did he want to push the dinner plates aside and scrawl in huge letters the next line of his tautological epic. Sometimes he would get so excited, forming the letters with his tongue before they came out. Like a child. Often the plates would slip in his excitement and smash on the floor. The noise would startle him but he was growing used to loud noises.

Every morning was the distraction of breakfast and his own mind before his muscles pulled him out of the chair, put on his boots and took him out the door. A packed lunch was always left on the counter for him. Without this he would starve.

Joyce was balancing on the second storey, on the edge of a two-by-four, pulling a joist with the claw of his hammer. Pulling a roof while he was suspended in air. Not the time for vertigo, but thankfully Joyce was half-blind and couldn't see the ground below him. He hammered in a couple of nails. He just missed his toe.

The boss walked effortlessly along the two-by-four and grabbed the hammer out of Joyce's hand.

"Only two hits. See?"

He demonstrated how to hammer in the nail using only two strikes. "You are too slow."

Joyce looked down into nothingness and imagined himself in the third person. He took the hammer back from the boss just as he realized the protagonist in this story might not be him.

Down on the first storey Samuel was looking for Joyce, asking the burly men about epiphany. They had no idea what he was going on about. His ashen suit was foreign among these hands. He had come to see his mentor, to pick up the bent nails and use them as letters, to find meaning in the structure of the house. Samuel called up to Joyce.

"What the hell are you doing here?"

"I came to hear of the next chapter."

"I'm nailing."

"I see."

"Please don't come here, Sam. I have been lusting after anonymity. My muscles are being discovered."

"Get to work, pencil arms. Two hits only."

"I can't talk. Come by tonight." Samuel left the order of the frame. The smell of the wood reminded him of pages.

That night found Joyce with broken plates on the kitchen floor. Shards of story. The doorbell rang and Joyce finished his thought, pressing hard into the tablecloth. The tablecloths were never patterned, always white. Joyce answered the door. It was Samuel.

Samuel came often because it was getting harder for Joyce to see. The young Samuel, his suit depressing, and the older man, his muscles tired now every evening, sat in hard-backed chairs. Joyce dictated, speaking to the air, and Samuel caught the words and wrote them in his tattered notebook. Occasionally Samuel would interrupt Joyce to remind him of a passage in Dante. This would inevitably invoke ire in the master. Joyce would often fall asleep in the middle of a sentence. Samuel never knew whether to wake him or quietly let himself out.

That night Joyce was upset that Samuel had interrupted his anonymity. He spoke into the air, but Samuel did not write it down.

"I want to experience the life of the labourer. Too long have I gone in my mind. I need to exercise, to feel the blood in me before this book is completed. When it is finished I fear I will have nothing, be an empty vessel. So I am building up my body, associating with thick-headed men, men with more than one callus on their hand."

"You could be killed. I saw you up on that beam, your eyesight is bad."

"I need not be reminded."

"But the world cannot lose you to a tumble from the second storey."

"I am getting old."

The next day the crew was putting in the roof. Joyce was still trying to perfect the technique of hitting in the nails with two strikes. He knew the crew boss was getting impatient with him. The other men were pleasant, but never included him in their conversation. They would talk about the night before when they all drank at the pub and O'Malley had tipped over the table in another one of his rages. Joyce had never met O'Malley. Joyce would eat his lunch listening to the conversation, trapping dialect in the net of his brain, to be used later in the manuscript.

It was a day struggling toward rain. A mist covered the frame of the house. On the second storey Joyce slipped on the damp board and tumbled to the ground. His glasses flew into the mud. The other labourers saw him out of the corner of their eyes as he flew. They ran to his side.

Joyce lay in the mud, wincing in pain. One of the largest of the men picked him up in his arms and carried him to the hospital. Joyce could hear the boss telling everyone to get back to work. Because he was blind, Joyce gave up his body to this man. His world was opaque.

Samuel would come often to visit Joyce at the hospital. Joyce had broken his leg in two places and he lay in a bed with it suspended. Samuel scolded him like a parent.

Joyce wrote in large letters on his cast until it was completely covered.

The Revolution

After Karl Marx was exiled he was forced to become a used car salesman, neon banners flapping in the wind. He had obtained his seller's license in Germany before the altercation. He always knew he would be forced to work to remain alive. His book sales had dropped since the exile. He thought about working in a coathanger factory but the hours were murder. Selling cars was his parachute.

He was shocked to learn that K-cars had computers, power steering blew his mind. The silver Jettas and bronze Oldsmobiles were parked in the lot, shiny, welcoming. Banners were flapping from their aerials, all red banners. Karl was the master of the soft sell. Let them take it for a test drive and then move in for the kill. Karl had no problem getting hot cars for cheap. The other sellers were worried about losing their licenses but Karl was a rebel.

Every interaction became a potential sale.

But soon a sense of foreboding filled him when a young couple approached a burgundy Jetta. He knew they would buy it, there would never be any question. Karl grew tired of interaction. He bought a dog, a Rottweiler, its tail short to hide emotion. The dog guarded the car lot at night. Karl called the Rottweiler Cindy because its head was shaped like a cinderblock. Customers stopped coming around because Karl let Cindy wander the lot during the day. He sat in the small clapboard booth smoking a pipe. He was tired of the soft sell and resorted to no sales at all.

One day he got hungry and took one of the Oldsmobiles, an olive-green beauty, through the drive-in. He left Cindy to guard the place, he knew he could trust her. Karl liked the drive-in because of the minimal human interaction. His exile had made him cautious. Karl approved of fast food because it is fuel for the masses.

When he returned to the lot with an arch-deluxe for Cindy, she had pinned a young couple against the clapboard booth.

They were terrified, but Cindy was just sitting friendly, drooling. Karl leashed Cindy and welcomed the man and woman into the booth. He made them coffee on his hotplate. Karl sat and smoked his pipe and asked them simple questions to calm them down. What they were looking for, whether the man had considered growing a beard, the woman's dress was pretty, was it local? Colours, mileage, distance. Of course, they were looking for a Jetta. Silver as it turned out.

When the couple had calmed down Karl suggested they go for a test drive. Secretly he was reluctant to make a sale, but outwardly he was calm and businesslike. The man drove slowly at first, but the woman, the two of them up front, insisted that he drive faster to test the steering, the brakes, the radio. Karl was in the back suggesting routes through the city that would allow some speed and maneuvering. When crossing Main Street the woman touched the man's leg and the silver Jetta shot sidelong into a taxi.

What seemed days later — but was only moments because a crowd was just beginning to form on the sidewalk — Karl opened his eyes and found himself slumped out of the back door. It had obviously opened during the crash. Karl checked the front and witnessed the faces of the couple enveloped by air bags. They were unconscious. A drunk man asked him the way to the old road where apparently there was an exceptional rib place. It was only later that he would realize this man was, in fact, the cabbie.

The next day Karl Marx answered an ad in the classifieds for workers at the coathanger factory. At his interview he neglected to mention the many books he had published on the revolution. Not since being exiled had Karl Marx felt so at home.

Intruders

What are these intrusive moments, like hovercraft gliding into view? These luxuries of mind. What are these tiny breaths acknowledged? What happened to the child who missed his class photo because he stopped to tie his shoe for the first time? These moments pull us back, make us conscious of the camera. They are moments left unphotographable and remote.

My sister and I play lawn darts in the back yard. My sister is baby-sitting me for the first time while our parents are reduced to a scrawled number waiting by the phone. Suddenly the gate flies open and a drunk old man enters. He claims to be our grandfather as a dart just misses his toe. My sister doesn't believe him but he insists. He calls us names I don't recognize. I have never met my father's father, could this be him? I run into the house terrified, locking every door. I strand my sister on the back yard island of the man's delusion. Then I'm on the phone with the sounds of a party in the background. All I can do is apologize for ruining it.

I started a n... b. It consisted of going to
building sets ...dio and
alterna... I w...ld spend
once writing the ...-by-step
instruc... ...d—done the w... ...before.
Althou... a reasonable eno...h plan, t...
...gon be... ...e in the theatr of t... absurd

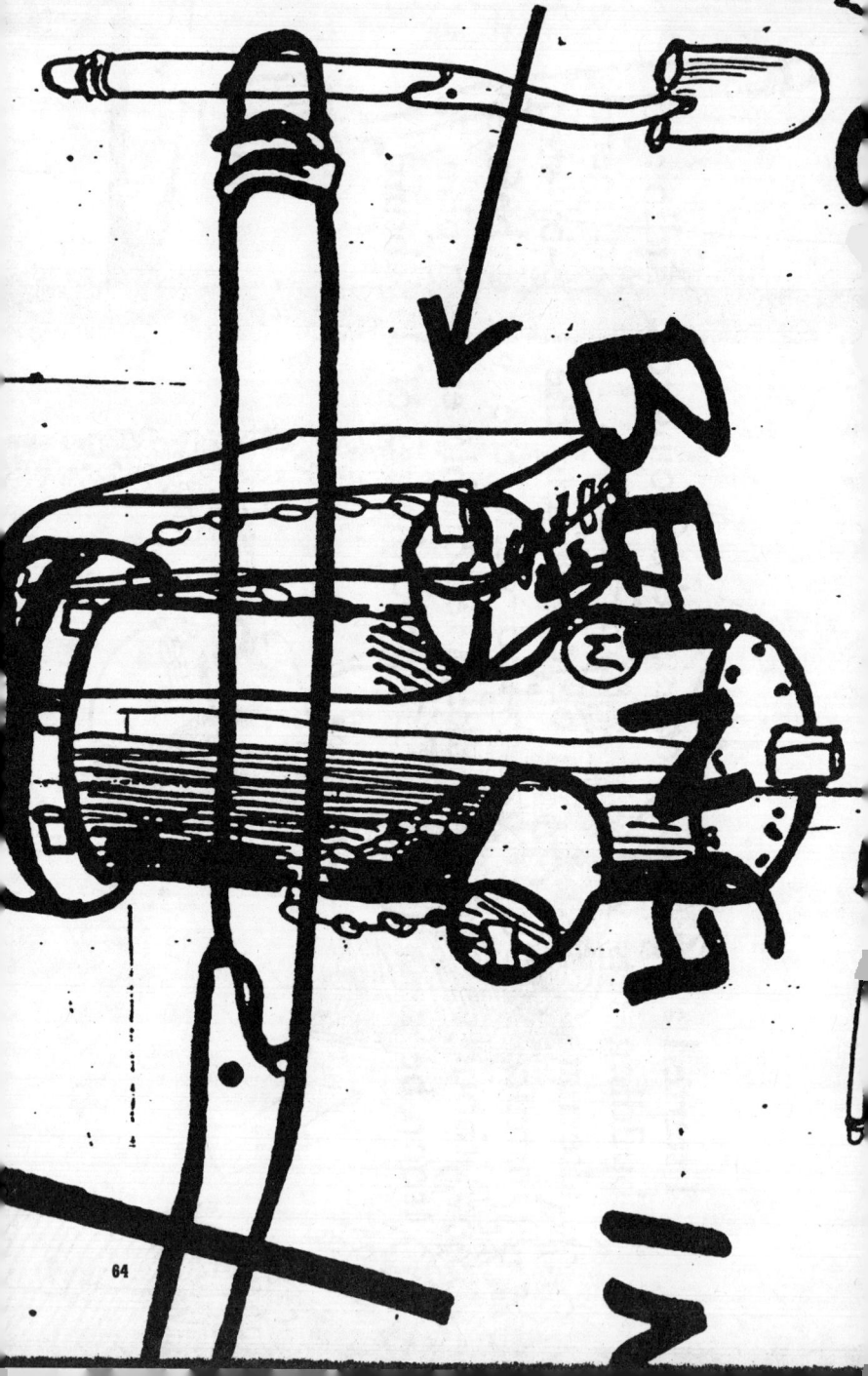

Everyone understands why we are here. We are all confidants at the clinic. Eyes are averted, there is tight security, men in cowboy boots and ponytails pace the halls. Hushed voices on the telephone repeat, "It's over." Beautiful couples hold hands. A family of four. A room named after waiting. The soap opera on television provides background. Tragic lives. Then suddenly the room is pierced by a familiar noise (anywhere but here) and heads turn uncomfortable at the sound of a baby's cry coming from the television. After it's over you will emerge exhausted, asking me to drive.

During the heat wave the chic coffee shops are packed with the nouveau riche. Then he lumbers into view, naked. His stomach is on vacation, lolling like a cow's tongue. But the patrons sipping *café-au-laits* are unperturbed by this intrusion on their sight lines. This neighbourhood is up for sale and he doesn't even have a pocket to keep his change in.

ugh it sounded like a
became an exercise in

They only stole my CDs which makes me think junkies. But I don't seek the plastic spines sequestered in neighbourhood pawn shops, because I am spineless, afraid of confrontation. Instead I listen to the traffic now, the hum of the vents below, appreciate the voices in the pipes. I learn to play guitar. Somewhere my music courses through veins.

After my grandmother caught her purse on fire my mother made the decision and enlisted us to help move her. She distracted her in the kitchen with tea while my sister and I carried the television out to the back of the Volvo. This was her most valued possession, the weight of history packed into the car. But my grandmother caught on, even in her condition, and came at me as if I was a thief stealing her tennis matches, as if I was confiscating her world.

He sits slumped at the bottom of the broken escalator, bleeding from the head. His winter coat is stained with blood. The Future Shop employees whip out cell phones. Hundreds of televisions shimmer above him, each one glowing with the glory of sport.

I ask the video store girl what movies are good, if my choices would be hers. I rent *Blow Up* because I think she might be impressed. I start renting movies I don't have time to watch, just to speak to her. After months of this routine, her schedule memorized, I ask her out. I had planned the moment for days. She says she's too busy, but I can hear the fear in the back of her throat. I pay my fines at Videotron and rent cheesy action flicks again. How long has it been since you moved away?

CLICK

I discover an old photo album and puzzle over my absence from the class photo. But there you are in pigtails, new teeth smiling, your clothes back in style. Shiny new North Stars are tied tightly to your feet.

Uzma & Isaak

Shopping for Contacts

Isaak had met the stranger on the bus before they disembarked together near the edge of the downtown core. They began walking in the same direction, which took them across the bridge.

"I'm afraid of heights," said the stranger.

Isaak said nothing and kept walking. The stranger was becoming increasingly nervous. He looked directly ahead with scared rodent eyes. His arms moved in a rhythm not unlike a speed skater's, but his feet were slow. The river was underneath, exuding the scent of sulphur. Isaak asked if anything was wrong.

"I'm testing myself."

To distract him, Isaak began to talk. He found himself telling the stranger all about Uzma. He pictured her for the man, an East Indian with owl-blue eyes. She renounced these eyes, because people would call her exotic, and she craved her anonymity. Uzma told everyone about her grandmother in India and a scandalous affair with a British soldier, but not even she believed it. Due to her anomalous eyes, or perhaps in spite of them, Uzma was colour blind. She only saw in black and white.

The stranger never moved his head, but Isaak could tell that he was listening. They were almost across the bridge. Striding now. Isaak imagined the stranger would puff out his chest for the final few feet, as if completing a race.

Uzma once bought brown-tinted contact lenses. Isaak went shopping with her that day under protest. He had to pick out the colour for her.

4½ on the Main

Isaak lived in the apartment for two months. Junkies stayed there before him and have survived there since. People knocked on the door at all hours to ask for drugs. The innocent door chime came to evoke fear. He sent away all kinds of disappointed people: schoolgirls, bikers, old men. The calluses on his feet from treeplanting disappeared into the hardwood floor. Sometimes his dreams were nightmares. The only thing in the fridge was water.

The shag in the bathroom was a hideous shade of brown. A previous tenant had obviously put it in as a joke, but Isaak, with credit to his resiliency, couldn't be bothered to change it. Some nights it would be so cold outside that the windows would form ice crystals. Isaak found that the light from the lamppost outside the window cast eerie apparitions through the frosted glass. When, after two months, he suddenly noticed the light illuminating a face drawn in crayon on the ceiling, it was like a mosquito sweeping his eyelashes in the dark.

Through his window Isaak looked into the bar across the street. It was called the Café du Pôete but no poets went there. In fact, hardly anyone did. The place was run by Ricky, who always called him Neighbour.

"Hello, Neighbour. How are you today?" Ricky would say loudly in his Croatian accent. The television was always on in the corner with the latest update on the events in the Baltics. The best song on the jukebox was twenty years old. There was a red pool table in the back which was the only one on the Main that you could be sure was available any time. He wondered how the place could stay open, until he was a privileged witness to the after-hours poker games in the back room. Sometimes Isaak was the only person in there on a Friday night, other than the waitress. And there was a new waitress every other week.

One rainy afternoon Isaak was alone in the bar and Ricky was drunk and molesting his most recent acquisition. She hadn't been there long. She looked Eastern European somehow, and annoyed. Isaak had no idea what to do, the situation made him uncomfortable. She wasn't screaming for Ricky to stop or anything. As Isaak was leaving, Ricky called out, "Hey, Neighbour. Don't let the rain come down." Outside, Isaak lifted his jacket over his head and crossed the street to his door, looking in the only direction necessary.

One night, before it got too cold, the city held a parade to celebrate its birthday. The doorbell rang just as Isaak was preparing to go up on his roof for a perfect view of the parade route, looking straight up St. Laurent. Isaak buzzed in whoever it was. There was no intercom, it was a matter of trust. Although strangers were showing up at his door for drugs, and they always left empty-handed, there was never any trouble. Coming up the stairs were the former tenant of the apartment and a few of his friends. They seemed to be in a good mood.

"Hey man. I used to live here," said the former tenant with a trace of a *Québecois* accent.

"I remember."

"Listen… what was your name?"

"Isaak."

"*Oui. C'est ça.* Well… Isaak, can we watch the parade from your roof?"

"I suppose so. Come on in."

The former tenant led his friends through the apartment to the back balcony, which connected to the roof. They looked around at all of Isaak's books, his empty liquorice wrappers, the shovel on the wall. Once outside in the chill air Isaak took hold of the dealer's arm and he spun around smiling.

"People have been coming here looking for you. The apartment below me was robbed last week."

"Johnie?"

"Yeah. Has he got some deal going with VCRs? I always see the empty boxes in the hall."

"No problem, Isaak. My customers will find me. *Désolé.* Too bad about Johnie." They could hear the music in the distance. "*Ça commence. Faut y aller!*"

The parade was moving south. They all sat on the ledge of the building. Isaak was concerned about the nature of their collective blood stream. What chemicals were racing there, unknowing catalysts for a four-flight fall? Isaak was sitting on the edge of the roof while a woman screamed, "*Les voici!*" in his ear. The street became a tunnel of colour, the brick buildings became giant screens for animated light shows. Isaak could make out Ricky below, watching with wide eyes from the window of the Café du Pôete, a new waitress on his arm. The parade passed and all the masked creatures of the city had paid the tolls which allowed them access to the night.

After the parade, as the group was leaving, the woman who had screamed in his ear was curious as to why Isaak had a shovel hanging on his wall. Isaak had trouble understanding her.

Later that night, as Isaak tried to fall asleep, he noticed the light in the window again. The lamppost was drunk. It swayed side to side, an old man hunched over, the brain still glowing. Trees had been replaced with this electricity, humming inebriated, yet maintaining balance all night. The wind in the city was a tired metaphor written in blown newspapers. As Isaak tripped into sleep, the parade's paper remnants lingering like the drunks, he considered the perseverance of lampposts and somehow was reassured.

Uzma sat on a black leather bench. The gallery was practically empty today. There was a woman with a pierced eyebrow checking out one of her photographs. She looked vaguely familiar but everyone at these galleries began to look the same to her after a while. The woman unconsciously snapped her fingers.

The idea for her latest exhibit had come to her one night when she first arrived back in the city. Uzma always saw the city afresh when she returned from treeplanting. It took a while to adjust. Some never do. She had looked into a ground-floor apartment window where there was a woman sitting in the dark, lit by the glow of the television. A Meccano set was a civilization in ruins on the shag rug. Uzma took a picture of the scene, aware that by using fast film she could avoid a flash, which would inevitably startle the woman. The window was a frame of light for her to develop. All her photographs for this show were taken through the windows of people who were watching television.

In one, an elderly woman was asleep on the couch, the laundry waving in the wind in the back yard.

Uzma sat and watched as people passed. Some read the catalogue beside her, chained to the gallery bench like a whippet in a supermarket. She had come to the conclusion that couples control these galleries, simply hanging off each other's shoulders. The security guard was suspicious of anyone who was alone. He looked for vials of acid in their pockets.

A man with lambchop sideburns stepped up to one of Uzma's favourite photographs in the exhibit. He was alone among the gallery couples. He held himself with an anonymous air, as if he were trying to be invisible. The photograph he was intently eyeing was of a woman curled up on a couch, the glow from a television illuminating her face. When Uzma took the photograph she had imagined the show to be a hospital drama, due to the compassionate look in the woman's eyes.

The man stood for a number of minutes before taking out an Italian calf-leather wallet from his back pocket. He pulled a photograph from the wallet and held it beside Uzma's photograph of the woman on the couch. It was as if he were comparing them. He stood like this for quite some time.

The man took a step forward. He looked at the title on the card beside the photograph. Then he took out a pen from a concealed pocket and copied what was written on the card onto the back of the photograph. He put the pen and photograph away. When he turned around Uzma recognized the look on his face. She didn't recognize *him*, she recognized the look on his face. She had seen it in front of many televisions. He walked out of the gallery as if he were turning off the channel for the night. She almost expected the national anthem. Perhaps it was because Uzma was listening for something that her ears picked up the faint rhythm of the woman with the pierced eyebrow as she expertly snapped her fingers in the other room.

Uzma was five years old when she realized she was colour blind. Her father was in the back yard talking to the rain again. Her mother was inside the house preparing the flowers for dinner that night. She put petals in all their meals. Uzma sat in the wagon beside the chicken coop. The chickens were inside laying eggs and making a lot of noise. When she collected eggs it was like being swarmed by feathers. The sunlight kept the feather dust afloat. It was in there, in that chaos, that she practiced her sight.

Squeezed into the wagon, Uzma wasn't listening to her father, but she heard the rain's reply, over and over. He turned and asked if her red wagon was the proper colour. She gave him a confused look.

"What do you mean?"

"The colour of your wagon. It's the proper colour for wagons. Wagons are red. The sky blue. The sun yellow."

"What colour am I?"

He didn't understand the question. "Have the kids at school said something to you?"

With her father there was always a lack of communication. He didn't understand about the light in the chicken coop either. Uzma learned not to tell him about such things.

Much later that evening found her in the darkness of the closet. She was hiding behind her mother's saris. The smell was as strong as the chicken coop, but in a different way. The fabric brushed against her skin in the dark. She always came to the closet to hide. She felt at home in the closet, a small dark room with absolutely no colour.

Now, she spent her days in galleries watching people as they moved by her photographs. All in the same direction. Some of them had small droplets of water dangling from loose strands of hair. It must be raining outside. No one knew that she was the photographer. She listened to people's comments, watched the couples who needed to touch. It was only recently that Uzma had solo shows, magazine covers, articles praising her use of colour.

Galleries would never have taken any notice of her if she hadn't changed from black and white.

She came to the galleries anonymously and listened to the couples. She wanted to hear of the colours they saw.

Uzma dreamt of old furniture in a new apartment filled with dust and light. It was beside a drained canal, the grass squishing between her toes as the whole world came to visit. She made tea, then let it cool, watching the steam fade with time. Uzma poured the cold water into the canal to defend herself.

When Uzma was a child she and her father held hands over crayons. He described the colours and she gave her versions of grey. He tried to tell her about autumn, his favourite season. In Asia, the two seasons were hot and monsoon, but since coming to North America he had always loved autumn. They would walk together through the park on Saturdays and he would push his glasses up on his face and describe the colours to her.

Later, after he had died, Uzma held hands over crayons again. She went to Dr. Chrysler twice a week and he had her draw things on paper. He always asked her to draw things like her family or a house.

"Draw your family for me today, Uzma," he would say in a calm tone. Uzma knew these things were right out of textbooks and she did not want a textbook life. She wanted to live off the page. She knew if she put herself in the corner of the drawing or accidentally made her skin purple, he would stroke his beard and say, "Isn't that interesting?"

In the third session she broke down crying while trying to draw a dog. She had to admit that, not only had she never had a dog, but she was colour blind as well. Dr. Chrysler held her hand a little firmer and told her that tomorrow they would keep the labels on the crayons so that she could read them. Uzma felt gratitude.

Uzma told Dr. Chrysler about her father. About his face. About the jowls that were sucked down by gravity in that hospital bed. About how he had shaved every day of his life, never known stubble. About the black eyebrows growing longer and turning white. About the day he had bought contact lenses and how his whole face changed forever.

Dr. Chrysler, who had a beard, told her that he was fearful of razors. It was a few months and many sessions before she mentioned her father's drinking to him. As he took her hand he said he was not particularly surprised. Uzma laid out her intimacies to him like new sheets.

When she entered his office for their last session Uzma noticed that his whole face had changed. She didn't recognize him at first. It was the moment when Dr. Chrysler told her that he was going to another city and another practice that she realized he had shaved off his beard.

She brought home a picture to keep on the refrigerator at home. It was the only drawing from all the sessions that she wanted to keep. It was crayon on paper in varieties of grey. It was autumn.

In the Photo Booth

There were five of them in the photo booth. Periodically they would be blinded. Isaak was on the stool and an elderly woman was on his lap. The other three leaned in various angles like the branches of a tree. They filled out spaces.

While the photos were developing they chatted and introduced themselves. They discussed what to do because there were five of them and there were only going to be four photos. The old woman wanted the others to take them. A French man who wore impeccable shoes and round silver glasses would not hear of it. Isaak assumed he was recognizing her greater need for memory. A young girl spoke up.

"Perhaps we can do it again. How many will that make? Eight," she answered her own question.

They thought that sounded fine and the conversation turned, while they continued to wait for the first set of photos. The man in the glasses started to tell of his dog and how it wasn't toilet trained yet. The eyes of the young girl grew large at the mention of the dog.

The fifth in their party was the quietest. He had lambchop sideburns and, although he kept a serious face, his mouth would open periodically to reveal crooked teeth. He remained mute. He crawled in the booth with the others, a head and a right shoulder, then waited anonymously.

The quiet man's eyes scanned the samples under plastic on the side of the booth. He seemed to recognize one of the portraits. It was of a woman, about his age, and she was making a gruesome face. He spent the whole time they were waiting for the photos looking at her. As they talked about dogs he was thinking creases, the story lines in her face.

They all crawled back in the booth after the first four photos came out. In two of them the young girl's head was lost. To gain some height this time she sat on the old woman's lap. Isaak leaned in and tried to pull the curtain around his shoulders, with little success.

After the first flash Isaak noticed there were only four of them in the booth, making faces. Between flashes he poked his head out and witnessed the quiet man peeling back the plastic that covered the sample photos.

He slipped out the photographs of the woman, all four attached to each other, all four identical. Faces were everywhere. Another flash. Half-blind Isaak saw him rip one photograph off and put it in his wallet. Another flash.

The four climbed out of the booth to wait again. The quiet man with the lambchops was gone.

"But we didn't need to do it again," said the young girl, "there are only four of us now."

They waited until the second set was developed and then took their pick. Isaak only took one, the others took two, and the young girl took the three in which she was visible.

In Isaak's photo the quiet man is above his head, his face a map of time. He keeps it in his wallet.

None and Buckley's

Isaak spent the day at the track, shuffling among the real estate agents who scratched their stomachs and assessed the odds. Small women in knitted caps studied the forms or concentrated on the television screens as if they were about to escape. A portly man with binoculars smoking a fifty-cent cigar yelled at the beasts.

Isaak chose to bet on *None&Buckleys* in the fifth. The jockey had been exceptional years ago, until he retired from racing to become a real estate agent. Prospective buyers never took him seriously, however, due to his diminutive stature. This was to be the jockey's comeback race. Isaak wasn't used to letting sentiment get in the way of a bet, but the coincidence was too strong. "None and Buckley's" was what Ben used to say.

*

An old blue Valiant station wagon stopped to pick Isaak up just outside a southern Australian grape-growing town. As he put his pack in the back seat he noticed apprehensively the open can of beer cradled in the driver's lap.

His name was Ben and after an enthusiastic greeting they established that they were both broke and looking for grape-picking work. They decided it would be easier if they stuck together and applied to farms as a team, one person for each side of the vine. Ben had a friend in Loxton who he thought could help them. En route, Ben went out of his way to stop at every one-store town and have a beer, "And a schooner to go please, mate." Half-way there he passed out in the passenger seat, his stubby toes up on the dash, forcing Isaak to drive. They waited in the pub in Loxton until his friend finally arrived, looking reluctant, then left again with Ben in tow. He threw Isaak the keys.

"Why don't ya sleep in the car tonight?"

Isaak parked by the river, just out of sight of the tiny ferry service dock. The vents were left open in the Valiant to provide air, but they let in the mosquitoes as well. Isaak slept poorly and met Ben in the pub the next day. He stayed with Ben for the next two months because he had no way to get back to Canada unless he saved some money, and Ben could always convince him that he knew where to find it. Besides, he had transportation. In his desperation Isaak hoped Ben could be his parachute but he became his albatross instead.

*

None&Buckleys was at 18-1 with only a few minutes to post. Isaak put down one hundred dollars to win. The man at the betting booth didn't look up as the slip of paper popped out of the machine. The anonymous grey crowd studied programs that they twisted in their hands. Numbers tumbled in their heads like socks in a dryer, waiting to be lost. They ate sausages covered in mustard and watched the shimmering horses with coats polished like wood. The pace truck let the gate pull away and the trotters were off.

*

Apparently Ben had said something to his friend's wife, and now he and Isaak were forced to camp beside the Murray River. Isaak slept in a tent and Ben slept in the back of the Valiant listening to cricket matches on the radio late into the night. For a week Isaak ate peanut butter and jam sandwiches while Ben used the bread as bait to catch crawdaddies from the brown river.

There was a bird sanctuary across the river. At night the cockatoos would screech them to sleep.

"Imagine what all those birds are worth," was what Ben said.

They finally started working on a farm and were able to afford a trailer. By the early afternoon temperatures would rise to 40° C and they'd have to quit early to avoid sunstroke. To get a full day in picking began just as it got light enough to see the vines. Every dark morning on the way to the farm Ben would stop at the 24-hour drive-through liquor store. "Hair of the dog," he would always say as he picked up change from the passenger side floor. This is where he would throw his spare coins. Through the small take-out window Ben ordered two cans of lager and paid the bleary-eyed cashier.

"You've got two chances, mate: None and Buckley's," was one of his expressions. He told Isaak the story to fill the spaces in their conversation as they slowly covered the rural roads in the Valiant. Outside the window the passing landscape was a snapshot for the wall of a Buddhist.

Buckley was a convict in the early days of colonial Australia. He would develop an elaborate scheme for freedom and confide in only one other prisoner. The fateful day would arrive and they'd work together to pull off the dramatic escape. They would not rest until they were deep into the desert. Then Buckley would build up a fire and suggest his partner sleep while he kept watch. With his powerful hands Buckley would then strangle the thrashing victim, all his dreams of freedom aborted. Buckley would then proceed to devour the corpse, after roasting it over the fire. The next day he would return to the prison to get himself captured again, only to repeat the cycle.

Isaak stood in the crimson soil, damp from morning, and placed a bucket down between his legs. With rapidly searching fingers he pulled every bit of colour from between the sticky leaves and dropped the grape bunches into the bucket until it was full. Fifty dollars a ton. He managed to save a little every week for a ticket back to Canada. Over the vines they talked, mostly Ben. He unfolded his past like sections of a foreign newspaper.

"I was sitting for a while yesterday watching the cockatoos. It got me thinking. There is the city life, this life, and the life they have: playing, fucking, shitting in the water, flying around, saying something in a squawk when they're disturbed. Fuck, it would be good to be a cockatoo!"

*

They were the only two collecting after the race. Isaak was surprised to see him. *None&Buckleys* had come in by a length. Ben was wearing a light raincoat, even though it hadn't rained since the morning. Somehow he had managed to spill orange liquid on its sleeve. Isaak didn't recognize him at first without the tan. They marveled at the coincidence.

Isaak knew he was expected to buy Ben a drink or two, since his winnings were more significant. The past was sticking in his throat like a burr, and he found himself welcoming the opportunity to wash it away. Besides, he had a nagging desire for closure.

The bar was tucked into a back corner, behind the video library of past races. Ben filled in the last two years while bilingual numbers blared over the loudspeaker. There were other races, from distant countries, flickering on the big screen televisions.

"Why did you come to Montreal?"

"Well mate, it's a bit of a story. It's about a Sheila."

"A woman?"

"S'trewth. I met her not long after living with you. Ya see, I started travelin' the fruit circuit. Pears in Goondiwindi, bananas in Ravenshoe. I met her picking pears. Christ mate, she was a looka. We slept in a tent together, I even quit the hair of the dog for a while. She could barely speak English but that didn't matter too much to me, if ya know what I mean. She just sorta left one day. It wasn't that I came looking fer her, which is what you probably think. I remembered what you said about Canada being the cold version of Aussie. Do ya remember when I told ya how if there'd be a war, Australians would know how to survive cause they'd go bush. Go walkabout for a while till things cleared over?"

"Not really."

"You said that you couldn't go walkabout for too long in Canada because the winter'd kill ya. Well mate, I started thinking about the winter. About how I'd never seen snow. Imagine that, mate. Never seen snow. The air outside is getting cold so I reckon it won't be long. Some nights I can see my breath. It's like in those bloody cartoons, with the words coming out of people's mouths in bubbles. So, with this whole thing with Geneviève, that was her name, combined with my sudden..." he searched the air in front of him for the word "... realization, I took the money I hadn't drunk, and came to Montreal."

"Did you find Geneviève?"

"Naw, mate."

Eventually Isaak took off while Ben was in the bathroom. Everyone else in the bar was in amber, trapped like specimens, slowly sipping beer. The crowds had gone. The strays picked up the dropped ticket stubs that littered the place and compared them to the racing form for the day, hoping someone had made a mistake. On his way out to the parking lot, Isaak passed by a bedraggled stray whose fingers were covered in rubbed-off ink. This man was incredibly focused. He picked up a discarded ticket, shifted his glasses down from his forehead to read, registered disappointment on his face, tossed the useless piece of paper to the ground, and replaced his glasses on top of his head again. He had his routine like anyone else.

For Isaak, seeing Ben again made him feel like a fisherman pulling up his net, the spaces filled with wriggling life about to die. Dredging the bottom.

*

The picking season was coming to a close because some inspector had found a fruit fly. The bugs were not indigenous to the area and a ripple of fear washed over the pubs and trailer parks where the pickers gathered. The whole area was quarantined. It was time to return to Adelaide.

They arrived at a cream-coloured two storey house on a block with a video rental store on the corner. Ben had lost the keys. "They must have fallen out of my pocket," he said. Isaak just wanted to get inside and sleep, but Ben was seeing how far he could hold him. He claimed it was his parent's house but he was difficult to trust with information about ownership.

"Sit down with me, mate." He sat on the concrete step. There was a line of browning weeds pushing through a small crack.

"I'm tired, Ben. I just want to go inside and sleep." Isaak was standing over him.

"Thar's a spare hidden in the bushes somewhere. Later. Listen ta me first."

Isaak poked around in the bushes until Ben started to cry.

"Why do I do it?" He was sobbing into his stained hands. Stained from tobacco and the resin from the grape vines which turned brown and sticky. Clothes started to look as if they were used to clean out a pipe.

"Got a cigarette, mate?"

"You know I don't smoke. I'll just find the key. Why is it in the bushes anyway?"

"If it's in the grass it might fuck up the lawn mower."

Isaak continued to search in the underbrush for a way through the next door.

The next day Ben took Isaak to an apartment in the Adelaide suburbs where his friend Chris lived alone with his two cats.

"It's just me and the cats here," Chris said when they arrived.

The three of them sat in his very clean apartment, drinking from boxes of wine. Ben sputtered smoke as he talked, the ash from his cigarette perpetually about to fall. As they chatted Isaak's foot twitched nervously.

They drank wine, and Chris and Ben rambled on about their glory days of youth. The pranks, the sports, the girls. Then Ben demanded that Isaak see Chris' scar from Vietnam. His stomach had been wounded and it looked as if there wasn't enough skin to cover it back up.

After the white was gone and they were into the red, things broke apart. Chris started to weep uncontrollably about what he had done in Vietnam, horrible things, while Ben told jokes.

Ben wanted to arm wrestle, "Two chances, mate: None and Buckley's." He was so drunk that Isaak easily beat him. He became irate, so Isaak let him win the next time. This tactic also failed. Ben pounded his fists bloody on the table in anger. He wanted to fight. It was at this point that Isaak felt gripped by the sudden realization that Ben had become his Buckley. The kitchen walls faded away and they were now facing each other down over a desert fire.

Chris tried to diffuse the situation but was obviously familiar with Ben's behaviour. Isaak fled before the tears of frustration came to his eyes. All Chris could say as Isaak went out the door and into the evening was that it was just him and his cats, come back any time. Isaak roamed the streets of Adelaide all night. As soon as it was light enough to see he was out on the road with his thumb pointing at the sky.

*

Soon Ben realized that Isaak was not coming back to the table. His only remnants were a ring of condensation and a scrunched napkin. Ben had wanted to hit him up for fifty bucks but had missed his chance. The huge glass windows of the bar looked out over the dirt oval, now being circumnavigated by trucks pulling rakes. He thought it strange Isaak would take off like that. But then he had always found Isaak very unassuming in a disturbingly quiet kind of way. Like a piece of fruit conspiring in the bowl with the wax fakes. Then one day it rots and the disguise becomes ridiculous.

At the track Ben always searched the crowds for Geneviève but she was never there. She was not the type to gamble. The crowd made the loneliness dissipate for a few hours. It was the final race of the season at Blue Bonnets and *Taxidermy Bound* was coming up from the pack. Ben had taken the risk at 9-1 even though the favourite was the best in the field through the colder weather. He had been evicted and was spending his nights at the YMCA because it was getting too cold to sleep outside. The trotters were in the final stretch and *Taxidermy Bound* was catching the favourite. Legs and numbers rushed through his mind, the equine rumble, then the flash of the photo. The anticipation of the crowd was thick as it developed. The announcement declared the favourite to be the winner.

"Fuck," he said to himself.

As Ben flung his crisp piece of paper to the ground he was startled by the sight of the foreign white flakes just beginning to settle there.

Doing Time

The time pusher took pictures but developed obsessions. He was working the photo booth at the Guy/Concordia Metro station the day Ursula needed passport photos. She just wanted to leave, to go anywhere, and her passport had expired. After the four flashes she stood waiting for the photos to come out of their slot. A man mumbled a question in her ear, which made Ursula spin to face him.

"What?" she asked startled.

"Are those for a passport, or a lover?"

"What?"

"Well the only people who go into photo booths alone want their picture for a passport or a lover."

"Passport."

"Well then you should know that the passport office won't accept photo booth photos. Believe me, I know."

Ursula was a little confused by the man's tone. "Oh," she said.

"Planning a trip?"

"Possibly."

"Where to?"

"None of your business."

"I'm sorry. I didn't mean to pry. Just making conversation. I don't get to talk much." His words trailed away as he spoke, as if he had just smoked them.

"That's okay. I'm sorry. I guess I should find somewhere else to get my photo taken."

"Or find a lover," the man mumbled through his lambchop sideburns.

"Whatever."

"Have you ever considered the benefits of time."

"What? Listen, I gotta go."

Ursula was becoming nervous about the man. It suddenly occurred to her that maybe he had nowhere to go and met people at the photo booth all day. She hurried away, up the two flights of escalators, passed the one-legged man begging for change, and into the light of the street. Students mingled with the homeless on Guy.

She had just passed the Faubourg on Ste.-Catherine when she remembered that her photos hadn't had time to develop before she ran off. At first she was apathetic, she didn't need them anyway, had no one to give them to. Then she thought of the mumbling man and imagined him taking the photos home with him, if he had a home. As she stood on the busy sidewalk considering turning back, she imagined the man masturbating to her image. She went back to the Metro and underground once more.

The man was still standing beside the photo booth. Ursula was hesitant but determined. She walked up to him and asked for her photos.

"Oh. I thought you had forgotten these," he said holding up the images of her. They were still wet from the chemicals. Ursula grabbed them out of his hand.

"You are very photogenic."

"What is your problem?" she snapped.

"Have I done something wrong?"

Ursula considered his question. She quickly came to the realization that she was being unjust. He simply made her feel nervous. The air about him was disturbing. Her face changed.

"No. I suppose not. Bye." And she turned to leave him again.

"Do you have the time?" he asked. She turned toward him.

"I don't wear a watch."

"I understand. Would you like some time?"

The way he said *some time* instead of *the time* caught her off guard. He must be confused, she thought.

The man with the lambchops continued to talk quietly, only now Ursula had become entranced by his voice. It was as if the timbre pulled her in. The man was selling her on the virtues of time.

"Have you ever wanted to have more time in the day? Ever desired knowledge without experience? There is nothing more powerful than time. Imagine being able to enter the fourth dimension."

Ursula found herself in the photo booth with the man and the curtain pulled shut. There were no periodic flashes. The man gave Ursula her first dose of time for free. Later, when she came to crave the confidence time could give her, she would pay. She exposed her shoulder, revealing a tiny whorl from her tattoo, and he injected the time. Ursula was breathless. Images of distant lands washed through her mind. The places she would go.

Ursula left the man and ascended the escalator in a daze. The sun hit her face. The people fighting each other on the street were anonymous. In the Metro the man picked up the four photos Ursula had forgotten on the chair and slid them behind the plastic display case. He thought she looked beautiful and wanted everyone who passed to see her.

Ursula made it home that day and fell asleep in her La-Z-Boy. She would return often to the Metro to visit the man until he got hassled when he foolishly asked a cop for the time. After that, he took his business to the old age home and Ursula followed him. For Ursula, this was the beginning.

She used to shoot up time but she grew old too quickly. When she was very young she got a tattoo of an Atlantic sea shell where her left breast would develop. This because she had never heard the ocean. She carried her home with her always, able to retreat into her tattoo whenever time became too much. She liked the high because her brain would expand without experience. Memory induction. She had memories that were not her own. She found herself recognizing people on the street who, when confronted, had no knowledge of meeting her. She discovered that she had memorized phone numbers which she was too frightened to call.

In Montreal, in the dead of winter, it is difficult to find green. Ursula needed to walk her whippet three times a day, so she always stopped by the bonsai tree shop. She would stare in the window for a long time, fascinated by the breeze inside created by powerful fans. The sculpted trees in the window held a pose as if they were on an Asian cleft breathing in the sea. In the spring a dark stain on the brick below the window would magically appear, marking out territory.

Ursula introduced the time pusher to Ricky after her first week waitressing at the Café du Pôete. Istvan was a man of indeterminate age with lambchop sideburns and difficult teeth. Every night, after last call, Istvan and Ricky would sit at the small table in the back where the red velvet pool table resided. They would play five card stud for a few hours, stacks of crisp new twenty dollar bills in front of them. Head to head. One stack diminished while the other grew.

This gambling made Ursula nervous at first. She worried about the cops, who were well aware of Ricky's drinking. Sometimes they would be called in the middle of the afternoon because someone had peered in the window and seen a man passed out face down on the floor of the bar with no one around. The cops would come and wake Ricky, feed him some pretzels, and be on their way. Sometimes the cops met at the Pôete after their shift for a few beers or came alone to play the video poker. Maybe they knew about the poker games with Istvan as well.

One Thursday Istvan came in with a woman who was sporting a bad dye job and looked a little strung out. Ursula was reading a magazine behind the bar. The couple sat chain-smoking at the table by the window. The neon Café du Pôete sign made the woman's hair look even more grotesque. Ursula asked them what they wanted.

"Fifty," said Istvan.

"Fifty," said the woman.

Ricky came in and enthusiastically pumped Istvan's hand welcoming him in Croatian. "And who is this gorgeous creature, Istvan?"

"Charlotte. A client."

"Better look out for this guy, Charlotte," Ricky said winking at her.

"Whatever," said Charlotte. "You the owner of this dump?"

"Manager."

Ricky suddenly turned toward the bar, snapping his fingers, "Ursula! Get these two lovebirds a vodka on the house."

"Thanks," said Charlotte, "I could sure use it."

Ursula brought the beers and the vodka and they drank. Time passed. The couple said nothing to each other. Ricky ran out to get cigarettes and a new deck of cards. The neon glowed.

Charlotte got up to use the pay phone near the door. Istvan went to the back table and took out his stack of money. Ricky came back and locked the door. He poured himself a drink and joined Istvan. Ursula unplugged the neon and the jukebox. The two men played cards, the only noise was the shuffling, voices mumbling bets, and Charlotte beginning to get belligerent on the phone.

"What do you mean? Where is she then? … Why are you such a fucking asshole? … No … No …"

Behind the bar Ursula accidentally kicked her whippet's water dish and the water spilled on the floor. Sometimes she brought her dog to work. Ricky didn't seem to mind. She bent to mop up the water with a dish towel. Charlotte was screaming now.

"Fuck you! You can't do this…. Where is she? No … I … She's my daughter!" Charlotte slammed the receiver down but missed the cradle. It dangled from the cord as she erupted into hysterical screaming. She stood holding her face as if to keep the flesh from peeling off.

Ursula stopped mopping the floor and ran to the woman. She thought she had been stabbed or something, her cries of pain were so acute. Ursula touched the woman's arm. "What can I do?"

Charlotte pulled away from her sharply and screamed some more. "Get away from me!" Her eyes were possessed.

Ricky screamed from the back, "Hey you! shut up! You're scaring the new girl." But Charlotte continued to vent. Ursula went back behind the bar, "Should I call the police?" she asked Ricky.

"No!" He grew furious. He lunged at the screaming woman, "Fucking bitch! Get out of my bar."

"It's not your bar. You're just the manager!" And she began

to howl again. Ricky grabbed her by her hair with one hand and unlocked the door with the other. He threw her and she fell screaming onto the sidewalk. A group of drunk Bifteque regulars, who were heading home after last call, picked her up and she screamed at them as well. They kept walking, laughing over their shoulders at her. She stopped screaming and disappeared down the Main.

Ricky and Istvan resumed their game. Ricky's pile of bills was half the size of the time pusher's pile.

"Two more vodkas, Ursula."

As she poured the drinks she regretted leaving the whippet at home. The extra company would have been welcome. It was shaping up to be a long winter, the treeplanting season still far away. She yearned for the season to change overnight, forgetting that in Montreal there is no spring, only an end to winter.

Uzma and Isaak lived together in a quaint 4 ¹/₂ in the Plateau neighbourhood of Montreal. Uzma turned the bathroom into a darkroom, ignoring Isaak's complaints of olfactory terrorism. Bathrooms were smelly enough without the added stench of the photographic acid. She also had a small space downtown where she rented a machine to print colour film. She was friendly with numerous laser photocopier professionals as well. Her photographs were framed on the walls of every room in the apartment.

Isaak had contributed nothing to the decor except the couch and desk that he had fished from the garbage in Westmount. All the furniture that people threw out in his neighbourhood was either infested or scooped up in a day.

He worked in the coathanger factory and lived off the savings he had accumulated planting. Uzma got the occasional gig photographing large Indian weddings. Besides, she could always turn to her father's pension money. Her family had been living frugally off the interest since he had died. Isaak felt that at twenty-three Uzma had not yet recognized her mortality, whereas he knew, at thirty, that he would always be the person he was now. He sometimes felt as if he were living in a house without windows, allergic to dust, and Uzma was the door.

He could almost forgive the way she always smelt of chemicals. In fact, he began to find the slight acidic odour wafting from her brown skin rather erotic when they lay together at night. He lived for the moment of her body.

She refused to go on the pill.

"It's a nasty drug, Isaak," she told him. "It changes women, it tricks their bodies, it's harmful. I will not go on the pill for any man!"

She bought a book on natural contraception and made hundreds of marks on the calendar: stars, circles, crosses, an asterisk. She bought a vaginal thermometer and began a chart. She wanted Isaak to read the book, and he did, but her coding of the calendar was never clear to him, although he assumed the circles were eggs. He kept using a condom, he didn't mind. It was the moment of her body, discovering black ringlets of hair under his nails at the factory where he made coathangers all day, that made it all bearable.

On a late October evening they sat in their apartment watching a PBS documentary on the mating habits of eagles. How they fly in circles to an incredible height together over the sea, then lock and plummet towards the water in a dive. They imagined the passion of the eagles before they hit the water like concrete, or break free satisfied. Isaak purposefully pointed out to Uzma the fact that the male eagle always returned to the same nest.

"We are not simply creatures of instinct," was how she replied.

Later they sat across from each other at the kitchen table, only remnants on their dinner plates. Uzma had the day's newspaper folded beside her on the table.

"It's natural, Uzma."

"Bullshit, as humans we can reflect on our position in the world."

"And what do you think of our position?"

Uzma stood up without answering. She cleared the plates and put them in the sink. She returned to the table and unfolded the newspaper. She began to do the crossword. Isaak was getting increasingly agitated.

"Do you think it's a mistake? That we're a mistake?"

"No," Uzma responded from behind the shelter of the newspaper, "it's just that maybe an open relationship could work. People wouldn't end up like their parents."

"But your parents had an arranged marriage."

Uzma put down the paper and looked at Isaak. "That's different," she said in a frustrated tone.

"So, are you telling me I can fuck other women?"

"Yes."

"And you can fuck other men?"

"Or women."

"Ah… so that's what this is about."

Isaak got up from the table and stood over her. He slowly moved his face closer but the gesture was devoid of intimacy and became oppressive.

Uzma was nervous but spoke with confidence, "I don't want us to get upset. It's just…"

The doorbell rang.

Issak left Uzma in the kitchen and went to answer the door. Uzma lit a cigarette. She usually never smoked, she never bought packs, only singles from the depanneur.

"*Bon soir*… Hello. I hope I am not disturbing you. I saw the light."

It was a stubbled man, more grey than not, standing on the porch. He had a trace of an accent which Isaak couldn't place, but it sounded Eastern European. A Polaroid camera dangled from his shoulder. The insects were swarming the porch light, forming patterns around his head.

"What are you selling?" Isaak barked as he reached into his pocket. "I've got fifteen bucks. Can I get something for fifteen? If not, then…"

"No, no, no. You don't understand. My name is Antaro. I built this apartment."

"Excuse me?"

"I built this building. Well I was foreman of the framing crew anyway. It has held up quite well." The man smiled at Isaak.

"I don't think I understand."

"I was wondering if I could just look around. See the handiwork. I am retired now."

"Um… I suppose that would be alright. Come in."

"That would be nice, thank you. I know it is a little odd. You are very kind. Should I take off my shoes?"

"No, no. Don't bother. Would you like some tea?"

The man took off his shoes and put them against the wall. They were practical shoes and Isaak noticed that they were well worn. The man placed the camera on the floor with his shoes.

"Uzma," Isaak yelled to the kitchen, "put some water on for tea."

"Oh, it will not be a problem, I hope?" said the man.

"No, no."

Isaak disappeared into the kitchen. He came out holding Uzma tightly by the arm. It was as if she were a kite which would struggle into the sky if he lost his grip. Her cigarette was still burning in her hand.

"This is… what was your name?"

"Antaro."

"This is Uzma. He built this building, Uzma. Isn't that interesting?" Uzma said nothing. She looked at the end of her cigarette. She thought that he looked like a man who would carry a simple black plastic comb in his back pocket. A comb bought from a man selling them door to door.

"When was it?" asked Isaak.

"Back in 1967, I believe we did this one. Around Expo. You're 388 right?"

"That's right," said Uzma in a tone which took no care to hide its annoyance.

"Yes. Your husband has kindly let me in to look at the place. He is… is… what is the word… *indulging* me." The man smiled at her. Uzma looked at Isaak the same way she had looked at the end of her cigarette. Isaak rested his hand on the man's back and guided him down the hall lined with Uzma's photographs.

"I think the floor is slanted in the dining room. See? Down toward the door. I've rolled a marble this way and it has turned around and rolled back. It builds up a good head of steam, actually."

"Really? Perhaps the wall has sunk here. I like the colour. Did your wife pick it?"

"She's not my wife." Isaak looked down the hall where Uzma was now smoking on the couch, "To tell you the truth it was this colour when we moved in. We were thinking of changing it."

"Blue would also be nice."

"Maybe."

Isaak left Antaro in the bathroom examining the effects of the photographic chemicals on the grout. He went into the living room.

"What's going on?" whispered Uzma.

"I really don't know. I think it's okay."

"He won't steal anything, will he?"

"Seems like a total sweetheart. Reminds me of my father."

"Your father's weird, Isaak."

"What do you mean?"

"Let's not get into that. Here he comes." She reached out to the man, offering him a tea cup.

"Tea?" she asked.

"No. I see I must be going."

"It's okay," said Isaak unconvincingly.

"No. I see I should not have come." The man put on his shoes. Isaak went to the door, and opened it.

"Is the building pretty much the same?" he asked.

"Actually it was only a frame when I last saw it. All I ever did was the frames."

"Bye then, Antaro. Have a good night."

As the man turned and stepped across the threshold he mumbled, so that Isaak could barely hear, "Yes, blue would also be nice."

Antaro went to the next house on his list. He had compiled a list of addresses where he had worked over the last forty years. Since his wife died he had been retracing his steps.

The three storey walk-up he admired from the sidewalk was one of his. He remembered that when they were sliding the roof on some new guy with thick glasses fell and broke his leg. None of the crew had visited him in the hospital. Antaro was pinched by a pang of regret. He debated knocking on the door of the building, he could tell the occupants about this man who fell. But he decided not to. Instead he took a photograph, a Polaroid. He stood on the sidewalk waiting for it to develop. He wondered if it would rain.

He knocked at the next address and was let in. He took his shoes off. He always did. He felt it only proper. It was a ground floor apartment where a family lived. Two young girls. The German shepherd chewed his shoe by the front door while he had tea in the kitchen. The wife told him about all the trouble she was having with the kids. While the husband went to the bathroom, she confessed to being suicidal.

Antaro was a little perplexed, but the wife changed the subject when her husband came back into the room. They all had tea while the two girls watched television. It was the fourth tea for Antaro that evening.

Inside, the buildings were never what he expected when he viewed them from the sidewalk. But then they had only been shells the last time he had seen them. Some he had completely forgotten. Water from the damp evening sidewalks crept into his shoes through the German shepherd's teeth marks. He was always amazed that people let him into their homes. "I must have a trustworthy face," he said to himself, although in his sixty-five years no one had ever told him this.

Outside a particularly grey condominium he stood for quite some time looking in windows and taking Polaroids. He would wait for one to completely develop before taking another. Framed by a window on the ground floor was a woman watching television. She picked up the telephone and spoke into it.

Antaro wanted to hear what she was saying. He took a photograph of her illuminated by the eerie glow of the television.

A police car pulled up beside Antaro and stopped. The two mustachioed officers asked what he was taking pictures of at night. Antaro showed them the Polaroids.

As he sat in the back seat of the police car Antaro suddenly thought to ask the address of each officer.

Later Antaro moved slowly around Ursula's apartment, while the whippet yapped excitedly at his ankles. He settled into the La-Z-Boy while Ursula questioned him earnestly. He was not used to such conversation, not comfortable with words. He exuded the air of a man who had endured.

"Uncle," she said, "it's been a while. How are you?"

"Call me Antaro. You are big now. Everyone calls me Antaro."

"Sit down, Uncle. Would you like something to drink? You look tired. Have a drink. How is Auntie? Please sit down. Let me turn off the television so we can talk."

"She's gone… been a year now."

"What? Oh, I'm sorry, Uncle. How could I have forgotten?"

Ursula stood up and fixed Antaro a vodka. She had forgotten that her Aunt was dead but she remembered that her Uncle drank vodka. She even remembered that he preferred Polish vodka. Her memory was selective that way.

"Where have you been out so late at night?"

"Walking."

"Walking? Where were you walking?"

Antaro took a sip of his drink. He swallowed slowly and contentedly.

"Looking in windows. That is all it was."

"Looking in windows? What do you mean, Uncle?"

"I don't know."

He took another slow sip of his drink and placed it beside him on the table. Ursula put a coaster under the glass. Her whippet curled up beside the man on the couch. The dog's eyes looked out expectantly at Ursula, as if she were about to perform.

"Two men picked me up."

"What!" Ursula stopped pacing the apartment and looked at Antaro. "What do you mean, Uncle?"

"I was looking in windows. At least that is why they picked me up."

"Who?" she asked in frustration.

"I just got out of jail. I did not want to call you, to bother you. I paid bail with the rent money. When I got out I thought, Why not go see your niece? Why do you have a ring above your eye?"

"Jesus Christ, Uncle! You just got out of jail? You weren't drunk, were you?" Antaro looked up at her and said that he was not and she believed him. He was never a heavy drinker, that had been her Aunt's territory. "Why were you looking in windows then?"

"I was visiting the houses I built. People were so very nice to me."

"Oh Uncle," sighed Ursula with a note of pity in her voice. "Sleep on my couch tonight. Let's discuss it in the morning."

"So nice to me."

"G'night, Uncle."

"Good night, Ursula."

Ursula was only an adequate cook, but Antaro ate heartily. He twisted his powerful hands together and sat in a chair. After dinner she would disappear into the bathroom. Antaro worried that she might be bulimic, although he did not know the word for it in her language. Antaro had noticed her growing thin, he thought he spotted grey hair. In the bathroom, Ursula would shoot up time. The memories flooded over her, sometimes she had to lay down in the empty claw-footed bathtub to regain her composure. She was forgetting the meanings of words. Wasn't there a word for that as well? When she came out of the bathroom she usually flopped onto the La-Z-Boy for the duration of the evening. She sometimes picked up the guitar but couldn't remember a single chord.

Ursula would sit on her couch growing older everyday. She was doing time like a felon. There were no clocks in the apartment but she could see when the sun disappeared behind the three storey walk-ups by the glint from fire-escape railings. Ursula was working on mind sundials. The days were getting longer now, soon it would be spring. Ursula contemplated the seasons and grew bored of them. They were too slow for her, like clouds, or like waiting for a cheque in the mail. Istvan had found a supplier at Sunnybrook Acres. Straight from the source, this shit was fine.

Ursula decided she needed some air. She put on her heavy coat and slipped on the icy sidewalks for a few blocks. The air was freezing, her breath visible. She passed people carrying packages, wearing gloves, toques, and sunglasses. They seemed to know where they were going. A group of Hassid boys were wearing costumes which included big white beards and straw hats. She wondered if it was some holiday. It was always a holiday for her, planting was just around the corner. She ended up in an Italian café to use the bathroom. On the door was a hand-drawn sign which read, "PEE AND POO ONLY, NO DRUGS."

Inside the bathroom she collected herself. Her brain was racing. She remembered playing in a hockey game but she had never been on skates. She had scored two goals. Where was this coming from? In the mirror she noticed crow's feet and grey hair. Where had these come from?

Much later, she was uncertain as to how long, she awoke and it was dark in her apartment. She rose from the La-Z-Boy, a tremendous effort, and went into the kitchen. She put water on for tea and sat at the table. It was only then that she stood up and clicked on the light. On the table was a book, which she began to read. The water boiled after she had read the first sentence for the twelfth time. She turned off the element, the steam thick in her nostrils. She made herself a cup of tea.

As the water became cold in her cup she struggled with her memories, wishing for a moat to fill.

She opened the door with an armful of groceries for dinner. Some watercress, an aubergine, peppers. In the supermarket she had chosen carefully and for colour. She liked the colours of vegetables. Ursula had volunteered to cook for Istvan when she met him in the Metro that morning. Hadn't she cooked for him before? He had jumped at the opportunity to become more intimate with his best customer. Being a time pusher left him rather lonely. He had walked beerily from the Metro and was out of breath.

They met on her doorstep with a kiss on both cheeks and a turn of the key. Keys and locks. A relationship is an endless hallway filled with doors. You unlock one door at a time until eventually the key no longer works. At that point you either turn and walk back down the hall at a rapid pace, fumble for the right key in a daze, or smash the door down with the emergency fire axe. Ursula entered her apartment, groceries in one hand, and unconsciously put her key back into her pocket.

On the wall in front of her were over fifty Polaroid photographs, each one secured with a single tack. Water could be heard. Antaro was humming in the shower. Istvan followed Ursula in the door. He noticed the furniture was simple and ergonomically arranged: a chair, a table, a ratty couch. There were only frames where doors used to be. He noticed the Polaroids only seconds after her.

"What is that?" Istvan walked over to the Polaroids. "They're all of buildings."

Ursula put the groceries down in the kitchen, which was connected to the living room. The whole apartment was open. The doors had all been taken off their hinges and stored somewhere.

"It must have been my uncle."

"Who?"

"My uncle. He's staying on my couch." Then in a quiet voice, "His wife died recently."

"Oh."

The water stopped. Ursula took the vegetables out of the bag. "Here, let me help you with that."

"That's okay," she said with a smile. "Actually, you can put the water on for rice. Can you do that?"

"Sure."

Istvan got a pot and filled it with water. His hand brushed against Ursula's shoulder as he reached for the tap.

Antaro came out of the bathroom. His hair was slicked back.

"This is my uncle. Uncle, Istvan."

"Call me Antaro. Pleased to meet you." They shook hands uncomfortably. The time pusher was surprised at how gently the burly man took his hand. Ursula unpacked the groceries and started to slice vegetables with an over-sized knife. She thought it best not to mention the Polaroids. Istvan and Antaro remained silent for quite some time, until Antaro slumped onto the couch. It was the gesture of an old man. Istvan was quick to see a potential supplier of time in this man. He felt that security was on to him at the retirement home. As Ursula fried up the vegetables for dinner Istvan began to salivate through his difficult teeth.

Antaro was still on her couch and he seemed right at home with this arrangement. Ursula was a little worried about him. What was she expected to do? She considered offering him her bed, which would leave her to the couch but then she realized that he would never leave. Where would he go anyway? He really shouldn't be on his own. She thought that he had grown deaf lately.

Antaro considered going back to Europe. Back to the life of a bee farmer. His thick skin. The sun. He ate what Ursula gave him. She took care of his needs, which were paltry. Antaro was growing a beard. He did crossword puzzles throughout the afternoon to improve his English. Ursula began to resent her uncle.

The Polaroids were too much. That threw her, and the timing was as bad as it could possibly be.

These days she would look away when she was talking to him. Look into the paint on the wall, deep into it. Talk of her day. Antaro sat on the couch listening, asking about the weather. She went into great detail about the weather so that she would not need to talk about something else. When she saw the Polaroids she knew she would need to ask him to leave soon. By cutting the vegetables she tried to control the situation. She was the one with the knife in the room after all. While they ate she told Antaro about the weather, although he had not asked, thinking bees instead.

"What's with the Polaroids?" Istvan asked him with a mouthful of rice.

"They are buildings I worked on."

"Construction?"

"Yes."

"So those Polaroids are your legacy, I guess."

Antaro thought about this. His eyes sharpened on a spoon, and it was as if the reflection had captured his attention. Istvan noticed his face change.

"Yes. I guess they are." Antaro smiled.

A few days later they were walking back to her place from the Metro when they ran into Antaro on the sidewalk. Ursula had never seen him so excited. He said he had just obtained a new couch for her. He was on his way to pick it up from a guy around the corner.

"Istvan, I need your muscles."

"Uncle, it's too heavy for you," said a concerned Ursula.

"Reediculous!"

Istvan noticed a strange liquid fly from the side of his mouth as he said this. Ursula pleaded with him to help her uncle or else he would strain himself. Come, come, signaled Antaro and they followed him. He led them to a building down the block. Antaro knocked on the door. As his knuckles hit the wood, Ursula remembered his door to door escapades before he'd settled on her couch. She realized that he was perfectly comfortable with strangers, because he had nothing to offer them. She wondered why he didn't ring the bell. The door opened and a small Chinese man in a fur hat appeared. He bent down to lace up his boot.

"Just around side," he said in a strong accent. "My son there." One of his hands left mid-knot to signal to the three of them to go around the outside of the house. Antaro said nothing. Everyone knew what was expected. The son had a fairly new blue couch half way out a door at the side of the house, on the ground floor.

"I'm the muscles," said Istvan to the son, who simply nodded.

"See, Ursula," said Antaro beaming, "my new bed."

"That's great, Uncle. Let me help lift."

"No, no. We men can manage. Right, Istvan?"

Istvan felt as if he were being tested for something. The thought crossed his mind that Antaro was checking him out, to see if he was worthy of his niece. Perhaps this was some old country tradition, although he didn't know which country Antaro was from. He had the type of face, the type of slow walk, that made Istvan think of the sea.

"We'll need all the help we can get," he said.

The small man with the ear flaps started giving his son

instructions in Mandarin. He held up his hand to indicate a specific angle. The blue couch was beginning to develop darker spots. It was snowing. The father and son squeezed the couch delicately out of the side door.

"All yours," said the man. One of his boot laces was still untied.

"Thank you," said Ursula as she bent over to lift.

"With your knees, not your back," Antaro snapped at her as he cupped his hands under the other end.

"I know that, Uncle."

Istvan grabbed hold of the middle but his gloves kept slipping. They proceeded down the street in this manner. Antaro was breathing hard, obviously finding the couch heavy. No one spoke. Istvan watched the snowflakes pass through the pools of the streetlights. The flakes glowed briefly in their light before disappearing back into the blackness. Each one unique, each one a story.

Ursula slipped a few times with the couch but caught herself. Antaro puffed out syllables in a foreign language, straining under the weight.

They reached Ursula's apartment before any snow could settle on the couch. Antaro insisted on going up the stairs first. He went up backwards.

"Careful, Uncle. Take it slow."

Istvan helped Ursula with the bottom end and together they hauled the couch into her apartment. The whippet was ecstatic to see them, its tail a blur of emotion. Antaro had already moved some of the other furniture out of the way. The old couch was nowhere to be seen.

"Where's my couch?" said Ursula.

"Istvan, come and help an old man push this over here."

"What did you do with it, Uncle?"

"I called the Salvation Army this morning."

"What?"

"They brought a truck. Two big guys. Greek. One of them had these strange patches on his eyelids."

Istvan spun the couch into position. Melted snow dripped from his hair. The leg of the new blue couch made a noise as it scraped the hardwood floor. Ursula threw her arms up in the air in defeat.

"Well I guess you're the one who has to sleep on it. Ask me next time before giving my things away, Uncle."

Antaro said nothing. He unzipped his coat, unlaced his wet boots and put them in the closet. He fumbled with the coat hanger. Then Antaro slowly nestled his worn body onto the damp couch as if he were a bear entering a den to hibernate.

"My new bed," said Antaro, smiling contentedly.

Later that night Antaro woke with a start. He had used a hairdryer on the new couch before settling in for the night, so it was not the dampness that disturbed him but a tugging at his arm. The man who had eaten dinner with them was kneeling beside the couch. He was working hard to get the minute hand from a clock into Antaro's arm. Still groggy with sleep he would have assumed he was dreaming were it not for the man's dank breath and his overwhelming sideburns, which Antaro knew his imagination was incapable of conjuring.

Antaro leapt up from the couch, knocking Istvan to the floor with a thump. In the other room Ursula lay naked, traces of the man's saliva on her neck. In her dream the sound of Istvan hitting the floor manifested itself into a car accident to which she was a witness.

"What are you doing?" shouted Antaro.

"Be quiet or you'll wake her."

"I do not care. What are you doing to me?"

"I was siphoning time."

"You are a strange man. No good for my niece. Out now!"

Istvan began to mumble under his breath, the same calming timbre that had pulled Ursula into his influence. But Antaro would have nothing of it. He was tired and angry. He grabbed Istvan by the collar and flung him toward the front door with surprising strength. The whippet, who had been curled on the La-Z-Boy, began to yap. Istvan quickly got to his feet and tried to leave. He opened what he thought was the front door but was, in fact, a closet. Behind the only hinged door in the apartment were the missing doors, stacked neatly upright against the closet wall. Istvan barely had enough time to register that this was not an exit before he felt a blow to the side of his face. The dog was frantic. Antaro's strong hands were clenched, the knuckles white. It had been a long time since his heart had beat like this. Istvan turned and struggled across the apartment, Antaro raining blows on his head. Ursula came out from the bedroom and screamed. Istvan's eyes were filled with fear as he stumbled backward into the door. Antaro was breathing hard.

"Stop it!" screamed Ursula as Istvan fumbled the door open. No key was necessary. He looked up at Ursula, the blood leaking from between his disfigured teeth. She looked back in confusion. He knew that he would need to avoid the Metro stations and retirement homes until she forgot him. Antaro's breath was coming in gulps as he fell backward onto the couch, clutching at his chest. Istvan slid down the snow-covered steps and into the night. The whippet escaped out the open door and sprinted after the man, hoping to play.

Missing the Whippet

Isaak woke in his tent, sore and exhausted, with the knowledge that he would need to bend and strain all day under the weight of seedlings. He slowly tried to scrape the sleep from his eyes. Half-way into the spring season of treeplanting and waking up was only becoming more difficult. As he pulled his clothes out from the bottom of his sleeping bag, where they had been keeping warm, he was struck by the fact that the whippet was not barking.

Ursula woke up and put her arm over Uzma's naked body. She just wanted to lie in the tent for a few minutes. Forget trees. Uzma was still asleep, dreaming. Ursula wanted to wake her and ask about her dream. It had become a ritual for them. Instead she recounted her own dream to herself as if she were composing a letter to a distant lover.

She would let the whippet off the leash while waitressing at the Café du Poête. Ricky had really taken a shine to the dog, and since there were rarely any customers he let it run around the place. A couple walked in and sat by the window. They looked very serious, though not about each other. The man wore a green duffel coat and the woman a hat. Ursula recognized them from the kennel. The three of them had responded to the same classified ad to adopt whippets which were finished with their racing careers. Whippets are sprinters, faster than greyhounds in the short distances. Ursula couldn't remember, but she thought the couple had even adopted two whippets.

She served them drinks while Ricky played cards with Istvan in the back room, a stack of bills in front of them. The woman wanted a caesar with extra Worcester, "Make it brown," she said. He wanted a *rouse*.

She asked how their whippets were doing. Her whippet could smell the dogs on the couples' pant legs. The man reached his hand down in a practiced motion and the whippet lay her head in the man's palm as if he had picked a plum. Ursula let them drink while helping herself to the complimentary peanuts. She told the couple that they could throw their shells on the floor.

As they were putting on their coats to leave, Ursula came over to clean out the ashtray filled with shells. The woman said, "You know, you signed a contract?"

"Excuse me?"

"For the adoption of your whippet. You signed a contract. It can't be let off a leash in a public place."

The man added, "This is not the sort of place a whippet belongs. You are not the sort of person… why would anyone want to pierce their eyebrow?"

Ursula was speechless. She cleared the beer bottle and the empty glass.

"Someone will hear about this," said the woman with an air of finality.

"Surely you must be joking?" Ursula said as they went out the door. She had only been working there a week. She went to Ricky and told him what had happened. He told her to come hold his cards for luck.

Uzma lay on her back, awake now, looking up at the squashed mosquitoes on the underside of her tent, the ends of her long black hair were in her mouth as she spoke. "I didn't realize there is a whippet police. Scary."

For the last few weeks the dog had slept with them but now it was absent from the foot of their sleeping bags. The whippet had become pregnant in an earlier contract that spring. There were six other dogs that came from the logging town nearby. Her desperate scent had drawn them. Now the whippet's belly was like an African beetle in a straw. Ursula had no idea what the puppies would look like. She was shocked to see her whippet get fat, the ribs disappearing, the speed sacrificed.

She had been missing for two days and Ursula was concerned. Uzma comforted her. She outlined her ear with a finger, her thumb pushing back Ursula's short jet-black hair. Uzma claimed that it was all natural, hadn't she watched the nature shows on PBS?

"I remember the first time I saw you," said Ursula, "it was at the tam tams in Montreal."

"On the Mountain?"

"Yeah. I guess it was between spring and summer planting seasons last year. You were taking photographs."

"I'm so embarrassed." Uzma put her hand over her mouth and talked through her fingers. "You mean you noticed me?"

"You were taking pictures of the crowd. I was dancing."

"I guess I assume I'm invisible when I'm behind the camera."

In the summer Mount Royal exploded every Sunday afternoon with the dispossessed. They swarmed over the grassy hill and formed groups among the trees. The drummers always crowded around the statue of angels with bras and panties spray-painted on. The air was heavy with a beat, with the thick sexual air of summer. Ursula had been out walking her whippet and decided to join the crowd dancing around the drummers. An old man played a purple saxophone. Tattoos, beards, beads, European tourists and Guatemalan skirts were everywhere in the crowd.

Uzma loaded up with colour film and tried to immerse herself. She had her telephoto lens attached. This allowed her to take extreme close-ups of people without them knowing, she just pointed at the crowd and focused in on a detail. She framed anatomies. Sometimes she would take a whole roll of one girl dancing, a picture every few seconds. The gestures she would catch on the faces alternately reminded her of Renaissance paintings and foreign tribal rituals.

Uzma focused in on the ring above one particular dancer's eye. Like a halo painted onto the side of a warplane indicating a close call in the air. She stood about ten feet away, slightly hidden by a young man leaning on a bike. The drums had everyone caught in their rhythm. The woman was dancing slowly, her body making the same circles over and over. A whippet was on a leash tied to the belt of her pants. The dancer was entranced and Uzma felt a twinge of voyeuristic guilt at so effortlessly entering this woman's image. Her heart beat with intensity at the thought of blowing up the photo later, of hanging the series in her darkroom, a way of surviving the winter. She took half a roll before feeling claustrophobic and heading up into the woods.

Ursula was still talking, "Afterwards we ended up at the same planting camp, but I was too shy to talk to you. I kind of kept to myself. You were with Isaak anyway."

"I'm sorry."

"Don't be."

Uzma, because she was colour blind, wanted to ask Ursula about the colour of her eyes, but she feared sacrificing intimacy. Her tongue through a hoop instead. Then their lips worked in silence together before they unzipped the tent and devoured breakfast.

Isaak found Uzma in the melee of the breakfast tent and sat next to her.

"Porridge as usual I see," said Isaak. He was familiar with her preference for porridge, a colourless food. The year before in this camp they had no need to meet over breakfast because they were sharing a tent. They had massaged the pain out of each other's shoulders every night. Now Isaak used Aspirin.

"Of course. Hey, your hair is all sticking up."

Uzma lifted her hand and touched his hair. Isaak felt the brush of her wrist on his neck. It was a remnant of a gesture between them, like a residual patch of spruce standing amid the destruction of stumps. They used incomplete sentences as they slowly adjusted to the morning. While Uzma made lunches for herself and Ursula she remembered that day in Montreal.

She and Isaak had walked to the Metro together. She was going to a new gallery across town where they had a few of her photos on display. Isaak came for the walk. The sun was shining but it was a chilly autumn day. There was a scraggle of leaves on the trees like the laundry of puppets. Isaak bent over and picked up an elastic band. He put it in his pocket.

"Why did you do that?"

"What?"

"Pick up that elastic."

"Why let it go to waste?"

Uzma hated the way he always answered a question with another question. She kissed him on the cheek when they parted at the Metro. His stubble was so long it had grown soft.

She sat in the gallery all morning watching the people look at her photographs. In the afternoon she had some errands to run. She went to see Mike at the photocopy shop, she wanted to fiddle with the laser photocopier for a project she was working on. As usual Mike let her in the back and gave her free rein. As long as she paid for what she did he just let her take control. He dealt with some other customers while Uzma tried to translate the greys. Mike came back to see how she was doing. She confessed to being colour blind, and he excitedly wanted to help her, show her which colours were which. Uzma let him. He was having a difficult time explaining violet to her so he just leaned over and kissed her on the lips.

"That's violet," he said.

Uzma let him show her all the colours he was capable of, there in the back room of the copy shop.

Uzma had kissed Isaak on the cheek, not the mouth, and it was obvious to him that something was wrong. When she came home later that night Isaak asked her what it was. She said something about elastic bands before launching into a wild diatribe about the mating habits of eagles. Then she went into the darkroom to develop pictures. Soon Isaak had to take a piss so he knocked on the bathroom door but there was no answer. He went out to the fire escape and climbed up onto the roof. His breath mingled in the autumn air with the steam rising from his stream. Isaak looked up at the stars and thought how arbitrary they were. He arranged them into constellations that night in an attempt to explain his story.

Ursula found the rain dripping from the hoop above her eye fascinating. The water clung to the perfect gold ring, desperate to become a part of her face, to be mistaken for sweat or a tear. Ursula hunted the ground methodically. The clay built up on her shovel and she periodically needed to scrape it off with her boot. This would cause her to lose her rhythm. She kept expecting to catch glimpses of the whippet curled on a stump, nestled in the tall grass with its nose into the wind, or wandering the logging roads, looking for a truck to chase at full speed. Anyone who had watched them together before would have been reminded of a circus act they had witnessed as a child. But now the dog was never there when she turned her head. She had to trust it to find its own way back, but she was not used to trust.

Ursula lay in the moss with her eyes closed. She had crawled into the woods to have a nap, leaving her shovel as a signpost for Uzma. She tied flagging tape around the handle, not knowing that Uzma would miss the bright red flutter in the uncontrollable green. Uzma found Ursula anyway, simply because she went looking.

The wind started to blow hard. Uzma escaped the full force of it when she entered the woods. No one ever strayed too far from the last tree cut. They had all heard the stories. Uzma settled in the moss beside Ursula without making a sound. With their eyes closed they listened to the wind.

Echoing the sound of the wind, the trees swayed at their tips. The trunks were doing a slow, methodical dance. When Ursula opened her eyes the trees looked like they were a concerned crowd peering down on her as she regained consciousness on a rush hour sidewalk. Then she heard moaning and the occasional crack. Dizziness overtook her and she felt the need to look down, where the trunks remained motionless, transfixed in the moss. It was then that she noticed Uzma beside her.

Uzma began to dream about her father. He was on a busy city street picking up elastic bands which he kept around his wrist. He was brought up in India not to waste anything that could be useful. Car tires became shoes. He was always picking up elastic bands. He kept them in a shoebox at home. Uzma would occasionally need to pull him out of the way of oncoming traffic.

Isaak stepped gingerly over the slash. He began to plant a line along the timber and then did cutbacks until he ran out of trees. Each tree was a comma, scattered across an ancient text, pages of land being written on. Isaak could feel his exact center of gravity because of the heavy bags around his waist. Muscles have memory. Waving a d-handle at the ground he was Chaplin with a walking stick. He felt like a newly discovered breed of six-foot tall penguin which constantly struggles to fly. He remembered seeing a copy of the *Tibetan Book of the Dead*, written in Sanskrit. It was like the X-rays of figure skaters the way the language read. Isaak's muscles moved like this and he forgot what he was doing, it was now all one motion memorized, like a useless physics equation in the back of his mind. It was now just pure time to think.

After his second bag out Isaak realized he needed to take a shit. He wandered into the woods at the back of his piece of land. He squatted, waving away the bugs with his hand. It was much cooler in the shade of the forest. After he finished he sat on a log the wind had blown down. His mind was racing away from the forest. He was thinking of the power of the media, composing letters to people he met on a bus, considering bears in swimming pools; he was thinking of women.

He stood up and began to walk further into the forest, toward an area where the trees appeared to thin. He speculated that a lake must be there. Isaak tried to imagine how many weeks ago the ice would have thawed. The lakes in the area were blocked with ice well into April. Water that could stop your heart.

It was when he failed to arrive at a lake and began to consider going back, that Isaak realized his mistake. He was lost. He listened to the wind, the crack of the trees above him, and became bitter at birds. He longed for a human voice.

He climbed up a tall dead spruce to get a better perspective on where he was. Perhaps he could see the clearcut from the tip of the tree. He was too frightened to recognize the irony in finding comfort in devastation. The tree waved in the wind but Isaak managed to climb high enough to look around. He couldn't see the clearcut but he could make out a stream.

Isaak remembered the old survival adage: when in trouble follow water, flow in its direction. He followed the stream as if he were on a Kindergarten field trip, tethered to its banks. His boots kept getting stuck in the organic muck and branches scratched his face. A few hours later a red flutter became visible through the green. Flagging tape! He left the stream to investigate. The trees thinned again.

Isaak caught a glimpse of a large animal lying in the moss. He shuddered slightly at the thought of bear. The muscles in his neck hardened. He slowly turned to see Uzma and Ursula lying together peacefully. Their bodies were respirating calmly in a state of obvious sleep. Ursula had her arm over Uzma's stomach. For Isaak, the effect of witnessing this scene paralleled the plunge into the lake.

He found Ursula's shovel, a signpost, and made his way through the cut to the temporary road. The van would be along soon. His face was scratched and his socks were soaked in his boots, but he was nevertheless relieved. Someone would be along soon. He simply wanted to hear a voice.

The foreman arrived in the van a little later and stopped in front of Isaak. He pushed in the cigarette lighter before leaning out the window.

"What the fuck are you doing over here? I dropped you off miles away this morning. On the other block. Is there something going on?"

"I was lost in the woods."

"Yeah, your face is scratched. I'll give you a lift to the other block. Hop in."

"Thanks."

Isaak sat in the front of the van as they drove along the switchback trail. The foreman took out a cigarette and put it in his mouth.

"I'm trying to quit but it's next to impossible up here in the bush. You smoke?"

"Not tobacco. Is that a Nicorette patch on your neck?"

"Yeah. Like I say, I'm trying to quit. The dreams I've been having since I got the patch are fucking unbelievable, know what I mean? You should get yourself one."

"I don't need any help dreaming."

Isaak was startled when the cigarette lighter suddenly popped.

At the end of the planting day, back in camp, Isaak peeled his boots off his swollen feet. Outside his tent he transferred his feet into sandals, then made his way to the kitchen tent for dinner. He maneuvered through the trees. Moss built up in his sandals, as if his feet had sprouted hair. Scouting the best path through the forest he heard breathing. He turned to see the whippet looking at him with deep brown eyes. What he noticed were ribs. He had forgotten about the bulimic version of the canine. It had seemed so odd when she was pregnant, like a starving child with a distended belly. Isaak was surprised at how relieved he was to see this dog.

The whippet moved forward and back, taunting Isaak with a purpose. He thought she looked slightly manic, her eyes not as docile as usual. She led him through the forest. Isaak was aware of the sound of the generator at all times, he did not want to get lost again. Whippets were not designed for forests.

Where the whippet stopped there lay a seething mass of fur. He couldn't make out how many puppies were huddled togeth-er, tucked into the moss. Isaak moved closer — tentatively because the protective mother was now baring her teeth. The closer he got the more white she exposed until she began to growl. His first instinct was to back away, his second was to consider the future of these puppies. Isaak pictured them riding in the open glove compartment of a rented van as it drove through miles of clearcuts. The clouds were cut out of the blazing blue sky. The puppies climbed on the dash and soaked in the redemptive rays of the sun, the land treeless as far as the eye could see.

Isaak backed away, watching as the whippet lowered her guard, nudged the mass of fur, and licked the puppies individually with her tongue. The new mother ignored him now that she was confident that she had a witness. He turned to follow the trail of snapped twigs back to dinner, feeling the need to communicate his discovery to others. Isaak made his way through the wilderness, following the comforting sound of the generator.

Isaak was half-asleep but he heard her feet in the sand. The sound of the waves were beside his head, just beyond the bright orange tarp splayed over his tent. Her feet stopped. He felt them sinking into the sand, tipping her as if one leg were longer than the other. Sand in toes in his head half-asleep.

"Hey, Isaak. Are you asleep?"

"Um… kind of." Sand in his mouth.

"Why don't you come out here and dance with me?"

"I'm sleeping. What time is it?" He opened his eyes but it was still dark.

The cook's feet passed along the beach and the sound of the waves gradually became stronger than the sound of her steps.

Later that morning Isaak woke in the filtered light of his tent. He woke to the sound of a damaged trumpet in the distance, the waves now barely audible. A calm dead lake created after the valley had been clearcut. When the river was dammed the lake formed. Consequently, stumps occasionally floated to the surface and bobbed. Along the shore waves pushed logs like bullies in the school yard. It was a hazardous lake for swimming, a stump could shoot up from the bottom at any moment. The lake supposedly had a high mercury content as well. No fish. The year before at this camp many people had been sick and the rumour was mercury. So went the legends overheard at the Mackenzie airport before the flight to the nearby airstrip. It was a dangerous lake where Isaak squatted. There was also an ant village under his tent, safe from the wind.

They were camped on a peninsula which jutted out into the lake, but a stream cut off access, so they built a makeshift bridge and called it an island.

It was a late summer contract, another escape. Isaak was hoping to meet some new people and erase the memory of Uzma. This new contract was a fly-in with a company Isaak had never planted with before. The contracts in the summer were much more relaxed than the spring, the clearcuts were beginning to turn green, which made the seedlings difficult to see, but the prices were usually better. It got too hot for the mosquitoes and black flies and the planters only had to fend off the much slower deer flies.

Isaak ordered his breakfast from the cook. She wore shorts because it got hot in the cook's trailer even at five in the morning. She had been up for two hours already. When she handed him his morning burrito omelet he looked into her eyes. He wanted to see if there was something in them betraying. Had she asked him to dance? Plants hanging in a third storey window those eyes, and just as green. Her legs were long but of equal lengths. She needed to bend down to hand Isaak his plate. She didn't look at him.

"Next," she said.

What was Isaak to believe? Had the cook asked him to dance or was that only a dream?

Isaak sat on a bench in the kitchen quonset. There were rows of tables with make-shift benches, just stumps and plywood. Isaak was afraid that sleeping on the sand every night might hurt his back. He thought about the ants and the sensation of their feet on his cheek, making a run from the bone under his eye to his ear. A trek across the senses. Isaak thought while he ate. He tried to adjust to the morning, the light filtering through the kitchen tent, the bodies bumping and waking.

"Hey there, man. M'name's Neil. My dog is Piggy."

"Huh?" said Isaak, startled out of his reverie.

"Sometimes people learn the names of the dogs first. Easier that way, I guess. Anyway Piggy's my dog."

"Don't think I've met him," said Isaak.

"A her actually. Well, kind of androgynous you might say."

Neil had a snouty look about him and Isaak thought that it was true what people said about dogs and their owners looking alike. Although Piggy was not a pig, Neil looked like one. He was a large man with his head shaved along the sides like racing stripes and the rest of his hair long and in a ponytail. His nose was slightly puggish but what was so disturbing to Isaak was the way he would look just to the side of your face when he spoke to you. As if he were talking to someone beside you or aiming his voice at your ear. Hotel patrons rented his eyes out by the hour.

"Is this your first time with Red Dye?" asked Neil.

Isaak took a sip of coffee before answering.

"It is indeed. You?"

"Ya. Came from a hellish contract with Natural Borders. Although I sometimes work for Blue Collar. Got in my bus and took off from that one. Long story."

Isaak took another sip of coffee to indicate that he was not at all interested in the story. Neil stared beside Isaak's face and ate some toast and they were silent in the increasingly busy tent, which was heating up from all the bodies. Their silence was like that of two strangers eating their brown-bagged lunches on the steps of the same statue in a crowded city square.

Red Dye was the name of the company running the contract. They had a reputation for paying well but also for being disorganized. The company had been started by a dishevelled man named Karl who did well by dumping many tons of red dye #4 off on the Twizzler's Liquorice Company before the big cancer scare in the early eighties. He'd made a fortune and started the company, since all he ever knew was treeplanting.

The cook walked by carrying a large pot of water. The water came from a well back near the airstrip, fifty kilometers away on a logging road, because the lake was filled with thermometer intestines. A truck went once a day to fill up the barrels for drinking. The muscles on her bare arms bulged. She was very sinewy, what he imagined Georgia O'Keeffe looked like when she was a young woman: long straight dark hair, potter's hands, hipless. He was afraid to ask her about the night before, worried she'd interpret it as a line. Nothing could be trusted here. Everyone was too vulnerable.

Isaak considered getting his video camera to film the cook carrying the pot. When Uzma had given it to him she'd said he needed a purpose in life.

"You're my purpose," he said, trying to be romantic, but she gave him a wicked look. When Isaak claimed it was too expensive a gift she told him it was an investment and was hot anyway. The view-finder was black and white which allowed Isaak to see through her eyes. He was beginning to feel a need to record himself for her. Isaak considered making a documentary on treeplanting to show the world what it was like to be tree farmers living on the edge of the world, on a peninsula jutting into a dead lake. The days of planting, of bending, of straining, of smoking were ahead of them. A record then.

On day one Isaak learned that everything he had once believed was a lie. In the morning the crew had a meeting with the checkers. They wore their bright red fully-equipped vests. Isaak filmed them as they demonstrated the temperature of the soil using an oven thermometer, like the one in a turkey at Thanksgiving. They were trying to demonstrate that the seedlings would grow in the warmer soil. Everything Isaak had ever been taught pointed toward keeping the tree as cool as possible. They needed to plant them on the sunny side of the stumps but must also keep in mind the snow and the slope of the hill. They must protect the crop by predicting the snowfall later in the year.

The checkers wanted the trees in duff. Who the fuck ever heard of planting duff shots for a whole contract? For the last seven years, the last twenty contracts, Isaak had to lay down a twenty by twenty screef and put the plug in the mineral soil. That seemed like the logical way to do it. Now they wanted the plugs part-way out of the ground and no screefing. Everyone was sure the trees would die. The checkers claimed different, tests had been done. Just when Isaak had evolved, his muscles mutating to the point where he had become an incredibly efficient planter, they had changed the rules on him.

Would you like to dance? Isaak was certain she'd said it. They planted a few trees in the afternoon. Isaak missed scalping the ground with his shovel, screef, screef, screef. He missed the cathartic violence, leaving scars in the earth as his tag, as evidence.

It was required that everyone have a partner because of the bears. Also if you fell and couldn't get up, trapped under the slash, no one would hear your cries for help. A partner could save your life in a clearcut. Good company too. Isaak's partner was Natasha the Russian Princess. Her skin was pale; even after ten hours in the blazing sun her skin only gave off a slight pink hue. She was the Dostoyevsky mistress, a girl from another age. She put her long hair in a braid every morning, a bandana, and then hauled the heavy bags filled with seedlings onto her thin hips. Isaak was constantly amazed at such a frail thin girl lifting and carrying the weight with such ease. He never told her this, he knew she would only have become defensive. She was a good partner for him because they planted at the same speed and they knew they could trust each other's quality.

At lunch time Natasha sometimes sat in the dirt beside the logging road with her legs tucked under her, perfect posture. She looked as if she were entertaining a suitor. Isaak wondered if she had ever been in love.

On the second day they took a break for lunch after their second bag-out. Isaak pulled out his handi-cam.

"What are you doing?" asked Natasha.

"I am going to make a documentary on planting. Can I film you?"

Natasha threw her head back laughing. Her lips were open in a broad smile. Natasha's lips were always a drowned shade of blue. She looked as if she had just inhaled nitrous oxide.

"Sure… I guess so. Why not?" Then her face changed to concern. Her faced changed as quickly as the weather up north.

"You mean, like an interview?"

"Sure. To tell you the truth I have no idea what I'm doing."

"You're fucking hilarious, Isaak." Laughing again. "Go ahead then. Film away."

Isaak pointed the camera at her and thought how odd it was to hear her swear so blatantly. He started to record. Natasha made a face for the camera. Between a girl and a woman that face. Isaak waited for her to become self-conscious.

"What's your name?"

"Natasha. You know that, you idiot."

"It's for the documentary. It's for the record. Where are you from?"

"Edmonton."

Isaak was silent, zooming in on the dirt smeared across her cheek.

"I go to U. of A. Came up here in the Valiant, the baby V. It has a huge dent in the front. Last year I hit a deer. It's surprising how much damage a deer can do. Thankfully I killed it, it didn't suffer. This is stupid, Isaak."

"No, it's great. Keep going. How many years have you planted? Do you have siblings? Have you ever been in love?"

Natasha took a bite of an apple. The juice settled on her blue lip.

"Forget it, Isaak. I don't want to."

She put her lunch back into her daypack then hauled her planting bags onto her hips. She didn't even use shoulder straps.

Isaak captured on film the Russian Princess labouring under the strain and then turning her back to continue working. Isaak filmed her first few trees. The grace of planting.

The physical repetition of planting caused pieces of his memory to loop like a film caught in a projector. At the end of the day he could only recall his tree totals and perhaps some song lyrics, while all other thoughts were erased. The next day the loop would begin again.

Bagged-out, Isaak noticed sky for the first time all day. Then he saw Natasha lying on a slope in front of him, her head on a stump, her leg twisted. Isaak called out her name. She didn't answer and he started to panic, started to think of the tiny airplane that was their lifeline and the one-hour flight to the nearest hospital in Mackenzie. He dropped his bags and went to her, calling Natasha, Natasha. When he was closer he realized that she was conscious but in pain.

"Are you okay? Did you hit your head? Twist your leg?"

She was on the verge of tears and would not part those drowned lips. Isaak just wanted to take her home and care for her like a bird with a broken wing. She told him to go away, she'd hurt her leg but would be fine. Isaak left her there so she could cry. A release.

Natasha liked to hide her pain. She lived in a world completely incompatible with reality, defying any assumptions. She was the lily-white Russian Princess, grinding away amid the destruction.

Soon, people started to claim that they knew someone from somewhere. They tried to place the faces from other contracts, from classes, tried to recognize the eyes. Uzma once told him that no one could separate her from her eyes. He wanted to recognize people but instead found pieces of her in everyone else.

Clearcuts became individuals after a while. Each one took on a different personality. The day before Isaak recognized a block he had planted three years ago. He had the creamy corner piece, which lasted him an entire shift. The crop was progressing, ready to be brushed in a few years, to form spaces between the trees to grow.

There was a barge that stopped along the lake, dropping off vehicles, food, and reefers filled with trees. It was very erratic in its timing. The roads had been flooded out of existence when the dam was built, necessitating the use of the barge. There were logging roads all around, a labyrinthine system of blocks covering the mountains, but there was no connecting road from town. It became necessary to trust the barge, a necessary dependence.

Thanks to the barge captain they had a surprise night off. The barge was late, leaving them with no more trees to plant. The conch was blown and everyone gathered by the fire. Neil carried a whipped cream dispenser covered in duct tape into which he slammed nitrous oxide cartridges all night. After inhaling, his body shook for thirty seconds and his lips went blue. He frantically scratched an itch through the stubble on the side of his head. Around the campfire Lao passed around his yin/yang acid and Isaak noted that he was probably not a very devout Buddhist.

Earlier that day Isaak and Natasha had been planting a piece of land beside Neil and his partner, Lao. Treeplanting was his meditation. At the cache on the road they all met up for a break. It was hot and everyone was sweating, their hats discoloured. Piggy was waiting for Neil at the cache and ran up to him, tail wagging. Neil bent down and thrust his face at the dog and in an intimate voice said, "Look at ya, Piggy. Come and lick my face, ya four legged handkerchief."

Everyone gave Neil distance on the log as he inhaled another cartridge, performing CPR on his idol. In a circle everyone was staring at the flame, tranced by the acid. Isaak decided to get his camera. The meeting became an event through Isaak's deeming it worth filming. The disco was back. It vibrated for miles off of the dead lake. Too late he discovered that there was not enough light. He continued to use the handi-cam so he could see through her eyes. As if she were out here on the edge of the rules.

The cook was dressed as her favourite fetish. However, she told Isaak that she was, in fact, shy. She had brought a Tickle Trunk filled with outrageous costumes on the tiny plane with her. Isaak asked her name.

"Una," she said coyly.

As she fixed her fishnet stockings they made small talk, used little words. She had worked for Red Dye for years, initially as a planter, but then had managed to convince Karl to let her be the cook. Isaak could imagine how she had convinced him, she held herself confident of the persuasive powers her body contained. He had already seen two different men disappear into her tent at night. She worried a stitch in her leather halter top.

"The physical strain was too much for me. I was worried about fucking up my dancing career in Toronto."

So she actually is a dancer, thought Isaak. He inserted another piece around the borders of the jigsaw puzzle.

"Not that cooking isn't physical." Isaak considered the heavy pot of water, the early mornings, the scrubbing.

Thanks to her trunk too much polyester was floating on the bodies in the lit kitchen quonset. The disco twisted around their heads like the Aurora Borealis, which was coincidentally absent from the proceedings. Isaak wore a purple blouse and a blond wig. There were other fetish dressers: an Elvis, and Caesar, the king of the Africans, was a cow. He played an out of tune guitar, trying to mock the disco pushing in from the night outside. He was a minstrel cow. The scene was a study in endurance, lungs failing from too much smoke and acid laughter, discussing impermanence late into the night.

Around the campfire, the moon rising and the back-hoe in silhouette, they created a story about a pair of pants that kept getting passed around from thrift store to thrift store. Imagine the bodies it would know, the surrogate sex pants can glean in the morning. Isaak put another log on the fire and went to bed. The circle remained in its babble. Isaak fell into his tent after negotiating the logs on the beach in the dark, passing through little Africa, through the woods, and along the shore in the dark. Night eyes. Not enough light. Even the ants had turned cannibal.

Isaak woke up with the feeling that something was escaping him, although it could have been the ants, which scurried away as he sat up in his sleeping bag. He grabbed the handi-cam and did a self-portrait. His stubble was getting longer, he'd have a full beard by the end of this contract a month from now. Isaak unzipped the tent fly and rolled onto the beach.

The water was calm, the mountains across the lake were patched with clearcuts. Instead of checker boards they were tortoises, too big to be turtles. A huge residual patch of spruce provided an eye. Isaak reached back for his Walkman and bonded with the ants and Glenn Gould's three hands. Logs from the clearcut lake piled up along the shore and changed patterns all day. He imagined walking over the driftwood, a naked Christ in a log-rolling competition.

Pretending to live a beachcomber lifestyle, Isaak arranged driftwood and made bone sculptures. The ants were under a binding contract to keep the bones a bleached white. He felt stranded on a post-apocalyptic Gilligan's Island filled with masochists. Treeplanting breeds masochism, pushes edges as sharp as timber lines on aerial photographs. Treeplanters are edge dwellers, slipping through cracks like milk through a hardwood floor.

The barge came that morning. Reinforcements, he assumed. Isaak could hear the barge captain's voice as he talked on the radio, the wind carrying it across the lake. His orange tarp was a beacon. Isaak had been dreaming of lemmings.

Some people had to replant. Isaak lay in the sun on the beach thinking of Lao and Neil, who went, as well as Betty and Veronica with the shaved heads. Working on the day off when the night before you were Elvis.

Later, Isaak interviewed Neil for his documentary. Neil was hesitant at first.

"Could ya cloud my face when I talk, pixilate my head, like on television? I would prefer not to be on camera. I served time once."

"What for?" asked Isaak pointing the camera at Neil, who sat on a stump in the sun, looking bored.

"DWI. Although Karl is spreading a rumour about me. That I assaulted someone. Personally I think that guy has a degenerative disease."

Isaak saw Neil in pixilation through Uzma's eyes. Censoring was necessary because people were vulnerable. Even masochists were vulnerable sometimes.

"How long have you had Piggy?"

"A year and a half."

"Where did you get her? Him? It?"

"It's an involved story."

"Well? I need fodder for the film."

"What are you going to do with this documentary anyway?"

"From whence came the Pig?"

"Well, as a puppy Piggy was living with these fuck-ups. You know, every day is Sunday morning for all they care. I used to buy dope from them and would hang around and smoke it. That's when I saw the Pig. The people living in this place used to kick her around and shit to make her more aggressive. You know, to protect the house and shit. One night I hatched a plan with my buddy. I went in the front to score and he went around back and waited. I claimed to be allergic to dogs and tried to make them put the dog out back. They just lit another blunt and ignored me. I insisted. They continued to ignore me. I picked Piggy up, under my arm, and leapt out the front window. It was a shock tactic. I was long gone when they came to their senses and ran after me."

Isaak lived in the suburbs of an African village. They came in a constant stream to the lake to bathe or do laundry in a plastic tub stolen from the kitchen. The self-appointed king, Caesar, aptly named indeed, frequently hit on Natasha. He was the epitome of smooth, the black Sinatra, the prototype emcee. Isaak warned Natasha about his type but she snapped back that she was not an idiot. The fastidious man who gave her Arabic lessons on the back of a cereal box was a devout Muslim, his tent was set up to face towards Mecca. The others from various tribes, various countries, all had Bob Marley in common. It was all they played, they took over any music by playing Bob Marley as loud as possible. This aural drowning started to irritate some people. Factions were inevitable.

Isaak went swimming. He braved the lake. He had to keep his head up as he swam so that he wouldn't hit the floating logs. Deadheads. Half-way out he panicked. He started to imagine a stump shooting up at him like a ballistic missile. He tried to keep moving but soon began to flail and became breathless. The beast of the lake was coming to claim him. His subconscious was in the process of acting out a bit part in a B-movie, but Isaak had to ride it out. He focused his mind, got his breathing under control, and started the methodical stroke back to the shore. He used his orange tarp as a guide. In this way he mapped his surroundings.

Obsessions began to form. He was conscious of Una in the corners of his eyes. Now and then he would sneak some frames of her with the handi-cam. Obsession in twenty-four frames per second. Isaak felt the blood race through him with the knowledge that he was recording her without consent, as if wandering out of the woods he had stumbled upon a lonely farmhouse and watched her through the only lit window. It had gone beyond the point of ever asking her about the night of the dance. He assumed it was a dream.

The camp was beginning to split into factions. The Africans, the beach dwellers on the periphery, and the *Québecois* cluster.

Isaak had flown into the camp beside a beautiful young *Québecoise* girl named Marie-Claude who could speak no English. She was extremely nervous being in such a small plane. The brown pools that were her eyes widened with every shift of the wind. Isaak practiced his French in an attempt to comfort her but ended up butchering the language, to her amusement. The pilot wore a hat with the logging company logo and had a tube fixed to one nostril which provided oxygen to keep him awake. He pointed out a moose, a speck down below. She translated into French for him.

She took the other French speakers in camp with her when she set up her tent in the woods. The men would follow her anywhere, although she was still at the age where she thought this behaviour flattering instead of aggressive.

The Africans took over a small hut in the clearing with FUCK THIS SHIT written in red marker on the single window. They continued to blast Bob.

Isaak lived on the beach, away from the woods or the clearing, with those who had lost their way. He suspected plots were beginning to hatch like turtles. What would happen to those baby turtles as they scuttled across his beach, seeking the safety of the tortoise mountains? Helpless things have many enemies. No one wanted to take leadership, but Isaak felt it was time to unite. Last night, along the beach, Moses had led them into the promised land with his Indian dress from the Tickle Trunk and a makeshift walking stick. That was where you could forward their mail.

Isaak bagged-out early at the end of the day. Natasha wasn't with him, Caesar had picked a special piece of land for her. Isaak decided to eat an orange and relax. He tried to be careful while peeling, knowing his hands were covered in pesticides, but the anticipation was too much, so he ripped it open and swallowed with satisfaction. He left the peels in an ash pit by the side of the road. He tallied up his trees for the day. He had done quite well, and stored the number in his head like a rusty bicycle in an attic. He fell asleep waiting for the crummy, the makeshift transport that was basically a box with seats on the back of a truck.

He woke to the sound of frantic honking. He opened his eyes, amazed that he couldn't remember his dream for the first time in weeks. He picked up his pack as the crummy approached. Caesar was still leaning on the horn and Isaak could make out the other planters in his crew pointing at him. As Isaak opened the crummy door to jump inside Natasha screamed at him to turn around. When Isaak turned he saw a large black bear with a brown streak on its stomach considering him from the ash pit. "When we came around the corner it was sniffing at your head," she said seriously.

"Looks like we came just in time."

Isaak spent the entire crummy ride back to camp trying to hold in his fear.

Surrounded by darkness, Isaak lay in his tent trying to drown out the rainstorm with Thelonius Monk on his Walkman. Unlike the French in the forest or the Africans in their hut, Isaak was completely exposed to the elements. He could feel the waves as they crashed next to his head. The beach was eroding. It would not be long before he'd be in the lake, together again with the beast that lived there. The tarp kept tugging at its foundations like a moon, like stitches. This storm would be its first test. Fluttering means the rope has become untied. Well You Needn't. Deny the storm. The rain pelted the tarp, background percussion for the piano. The storm was an onslaught, the waves provided the bass. MEGA BASS. The wind was a force to be reckoned with. The stumps were drowning in the lake and there was nothing Isaak could do to save them. And now Ladies and Gentlemen, the Rain. No applause necessary, it will provide its own.

The rain.

The rain.

The rain.

Isaak remembered once planting in this weather, just as dark during the day, and discovering the textbook definition of hypothermia on The Coast. The mythical land called The Coast was where the slopes were so steep they couldn't even be skied and the prices were insanely high: thirty, forty cents a tree. Needles were coming down from the sky and Isaak was running and planting at the same time. He tripped over stumps, slid down slopes, fought weather in a t-shirt. It was hard to believe that he had ever considered the rain comforting.

His tarp became a sail, taking his tent off to dream about the tortoise tattoos on the mountains. The storm subsided with the dawn, the batteries on his Walkman running dangerously low.

Isaak lost track of the days. Recording no longer seemed important to him. He used his handi-cam less now that he had run out of film. He used it now only to be with her.

In the crummy, the dust was a film on the seats, the air thick and sandpapery. When interviewed, no one could tell Isaak what day of the week it was. They had become unconscious of the camera. Through Uzma's black and white camera eyes Isaak saw Betty and Veronica, who were partners in more than the planting sense of the word, guess at the day.

"Could be a Tuesday."

"Ya man, it felt like a Sunday it was so surreal. Sundays are always fucking totally surreal, man."

"It's hump day for sure, dude."

The hair on both Betty and Veronica was the same half inch. They had shaved together in some sort of commitment ceremony. The hair on their heads was the same length as on Isaak's face.

The rookie lowballers planted two thousand trees while Isaak only got in one thousand. Flip image. Through the looking glass again. Seven people were fired, a full plane for the journey out. The pilot killed two birds with one stone by flying in some nut with a pierced lip and green mohawk to be a crew boss. The hierarchy must be established. There were no rules anymore. Isaak had the same dream as the last four nights of planting the aisles of a supermarket, the fluorescent lights interrogational. Stitching them in under the tiles beside the Nescafé. Each night he was fearful of drowning in his sleep, the beach eroding beside him.

Everyone must dance or they are fired. This was yelled at Karl in the swirling bodies of dance. Pagan disco on another night off, the second in a row because the barge failed to show up again. Some innocuous Ontario college boy in a baseball cap had to be flown out because he pissed on the food tent. Karl with his degenerative disease sputtered in bursts of anger, firing just for the pleasure of it now. It gave him a rush. A fear spread through camp of waking up one morning to a list of names, written in red marker, posted in the kitchen quonset, announcing the next people to be fired.

More polyester prints, more nitrous, and the bags of dope were diminishing into lungs. Simon wore red tights and a satin top and made some crazy gestures that had never been equated with ABBA before. Una moved her body to the rhythms, dancing unabandoned. She obviously had talent as a dancer but her cooking left something to be desired. The kitchen was covered in Silvicool tarpaulins and flagging tape streamers, like a cave of aluminum foil. And the disco, Christ the fucking disco all night. Not even Bob Marley showed his face, with all the suburban polyester.

When the barge finally showed up Isaak hid from the reefer patrol because he didn't want to unload the boxes. He wanted to preserve his back. Caesar and the Muslim alternated with Natasha. Some evenings Caesar played chess with her, a study in black and white. Other nights the fastidious Muslim was a teacher coaxing a child with a television attention span. Someone kept blowing the battered trumpet. The conch called forth the reefer patrol, who searched for those cowering in the woods.

Isaak began to think the French were plotting something none of the others could understand. They recruited the Africans, with whom they shared a common tongue. When doing his laundry on the outskirts of Little Africa Isaak overheard their conspiratorial conversations in unfamiliar languages. Isaak felt very underdeveloped and hummed to himself. He smashed his *Meat is Murder* t-shirt, with the brown shoulder strap stains, against a log in the lake. The cold water made his toes numb. The Africans befriended Pierre who did his laundry with them. Pierre was the main suitor of Marie-Claude, the beautiful brown-eyed girl. Everyone assumed they were fucking but no one asked. Days filled with rumour.

Simon with the green mohawk had a condescending attitude toward Isaak's spacing until he learned how much experience Isaak had. He sat on a stump and talked wildly to Natasha, who listened as she planted. His pierced lip caused him to slur. The batteries on her Walkman had run out so she was trapped by Simon. Everyone must plant or they are fired.

Isaak wanted to wake up beside Una, but everything was conditional. He obsessed late into the night, hearing her toes in the sand. Unconditional sand, it enveloped anyone but still managed to keep time. He was developing a nasty case of the shes.

She.

She.

She.

Obsessions like rain.

The clearcuts were the scars, the only reminder that others had existed before them.

The planes stopped coming. Karl couldn't reach a pilot on the radio phone. He said that this was nothing to be concerned about, as he unconsciously slobbered on his chin.

Isaak had complimented Uzma on her photographs. He used the words *charming* and *cynosure* in the same sentence. Uzma was flattered but also intrigued. Normally all she felt was boredom. Sight came easily to her. She just needed to record it and people would praise her. She made him always wear a condom although he claimed he was sterile due to the many years of handling pesticide infested trees. Later, when she gave Isaak the handi-cam, she considered the gesture as preparation for her disappearance. She timed the exchange for the first day of Ramadan. She planned to starve Isaak out of her.

Isaak did not have the advantage of formal ritual to exorcise the memory of her. He constructed an idol beside his tent on the beach, a Cyclopean piece of driftwood which considered the dead lake and the unlikely tortoises. This was where Isaak went to pee late at night. He tried to time the event for when Una walked past on her way to the cook's trailer. Sometimes he was successful but only a few words would ever be exchanged. He wondered if she was beginning to doubt the coincidence.

FADE IN.
EXTERIOR. DAY. PLANTING CAMP. ANYWHERE ISOLATED.

A Dairyland milk truck takes up the frame. It is covered in grime but it is still evident that on the side there is an ad for milk as well as a poster. There is a ramp from the COOK's trailer to the door of the truck. The COOK stops before entering the back of the refrigerated truck where the food is stored.

> COOK
> What are you doing? Why do you keep point-
> ing that thing at me?

> ISAAK
> It has no film.

> COOK
> Even worse. You're making me nervous, Isaak.

> ISAAK
> Posterity.

> COOK
> Oh, fuck off.
> (She enters the truck)

ZOOM-IN on the poster on the side of the truck. CLOSE-UP of the poster. A HAND comes from off screen and wipes the grime away. It is a Crime-Stoppers poster: 669-TIPS, like on the side of the milk cartons. The picture is a crude rendering but unmistakably NEIL with a mous-tache. The camera tumbles. When it hits the ground it points over the lake. There are tortoises.

INTERIOR. DUSK. INSIDE KITCHEN TENT.

NEIL sits on a bench with his head in his hands on the table. There are plates and food in disarray on the table.

ISAAK

Hey Neil.

NEIL

What? (Lifting his head) Oh, fuck go away.
I've had a difficult day.

ISAAK

Did you ever have a moustache?

NEIL

You ask a lot of questions.

ISAAK

Posterity.

NEIL

Some people have no need for posterity.

ISAAK

Handlebars?

NEIL

Ya. So?

ISAAK

No reason. I myself was beardless before.

PAN AROUND to a view of ISAAK holding the camera at arm's length. ISAAK now has a beard.
FADE OUT.

He dropped the camera when he saw the poster of Neil. Conveniently the radio phone was not working, and even if it was could he bring himself to call 669-TIPS? Isaak considered the reward and translated it into the equivalent amount of trees. The poster said his crime was robbing a bank with a propane torch. Isaak covered the poster back over with the grime, intending to tell no one. No sense in a lynching, there were enough people on the edge already. Luckily there had been no bears around camp. So far, it had not been necessary to use the gun.

Betty and Veronica dyed each other's hair in the kitchen trailer sink, Betty purple and Veronica blond. If Veronica became a blond how would anyone be able to tell them apart in the comics? Dopplegangers, those two. They partied away, "Partay man!" behind the whitecaps which demolished the fragile island. The waves stacked the logs along the shore to form a fortress around the island. Everyone needs some kind of protection. It becomes who you need it from. People wave at you one day at a time.

Days became numbered, not named. The dogs chased each other and guarded the caches from the ravens out hunting lunches. Everything existed in the figurative world. The literal was lost to the dogs, who tore and ripped it with their teeth to make it more palatable.

Ten people were expected to leave. A barge would be coming. More trees, more food. Karl was going crazy firing people.

"The longer the season gets the stupider planters get," Karl said to Lao for flagging a line exactly where he was told. Lao screamed back at him. Karl lit a cigarette and fired him on the spot. Lao dropped his bags and walked off the block. The crummy picked him up later, fifteen kilometers away. It took two days by barge to get to Mackenzie. Others quit due to the Kafkaesque nature of the contract. Everyone complained of the waits, the fuck-ups in providing land and trees, while still pulling in two-fifty a day, although they began to doubt whether they would ever get paid. Isaak hoped Neil would leave but doubted it. Neil had no license to drive his bus and no money for gas.

The barge came at night and many people slunk away. Lao was among them. The *Québecoise* girl who was scared of the plane was relieved to be leaving by water. She took two of the French men with her, but not Pierre. He wanted to make more money and knew that everything would end between them as soon as they left anyway. It was better this way. At night, while Isaak was dreaming of hijacking a logging truck to steal computer documents, they silently embarked. They left the island. Easy as that. Just a step onto the boat. Isaak sometimes felt the crush of separation anxiety when he finally left the bush and landed back in the city each autumn. One can become fond of anything habitual.

Amid the chaos of another night off Isaak discussed religion with the Russian Princess, who had been baptized against her will. Coercive, those Russians. You must believe or you are fired. It was becoming evident that there were more days off than days on. People were just refusing to wake up at the sound of the trumpet. Isaak felt like Gatsby looking across the harbour at the green light. But the lights he saw were the skidder drivers scarifying the tortoise blocks for the planters. The headlights illuminated their drunken paths. The liquor bottles were strewn about for the planters to find later. Isaak's light was running out of batteries, he was tired all the time.

Somewhere between the funky town and the passing out of the condoms, Una approached Isaak. She asked him if he would like to dance.

The land they began to plant on the next shift was sheer treachery. A river valley had been illicitly clearcut right down to the edges of the water, leaving many huge logs wasted and ignored on the slopes. Everyone slowed down, naps started to happen. Money did not seem so important when working in such life-threatening land. Isaak wore sixty pound bags around his waist while balancing on a log ten feet off the ground and trying to negotiate around the slash. Isaak gashed his leg, ripped his chainsaw boots, and broke the strap off his planting bags. The curses to various prophets became more prevalent but less creative. It looked as if all the cut trees had just been left on the side of the mountain, huge logs strewn about like a game of pick-up-sticks for giants. Balance became precious. They felt like salmon trying to scale a waterfall. Planting so that they could spawn. Passing out condoms wouldn't improve the situation. Dye-jobbed Bodhisattvas and their faithful companions screamed at the top of their lungs, complaining of the land, their heads filled with acid.

Veronica fell in the treacherous land and gashed her leg badly. The purple-haired Betty nursed her to the best of her ability, but insisted that Karl get a plane to take her to the hospital. Karl told her that it was just not going to happen. Veronica drank the last of the tequila that night and prayed for the barge to come.

Moses erected a portal on the beach to represent the boundary between work and vacation. If the barge did not show up it might become the only way out.

Isaak told Natasha about the poster of Neil and the fact that he might be a fugitive from the law. Twenty minutes later he heard the same thing from Simon. Rumour travel. The speed of information around the camp was faster than with fibre-optics. Of course Neil was confronted. Isaak took the opportunity to hide behind the handi-cam.

FADE IN. INTERIOR. DUSK. KITCHEN TENT.

The PLANTERS are all talking away loudly at the tables while they eat. NEIL is at a table with KARL and SIMON.

KARL

So what's this I hear about you, a bank, and a propane torch?

NEIL

What are you talking about?

SIMON

You served time right?

NEIL

Seven months for DWI.

KARL

And that's all?

The other PLANTERS at the table have all stopped eating and are listening.

NEIL

Ya.

SIMON passes NEIL the Crime-Stoppers poster.

SIMON

Is this not you?

NEIL

I don't look like that.

KARL

Sure you do.

SIMON

You do.

NEIL

(Laughing nervously)
Like shit. Coincidence happens.

KARL

Be on the next barge.

NEIL

(Agitated) And when the fuck will that be, Karl?
(Lunging at the camera)
Get that fucking thing outta my face!

ISAAK (OS)

This is evidence.

KARL

Just make sure you're gone.

NEIL gets up and walks away. He calls out for his dog.

NEIL

Piggy… Come here and bite these people, ya
vicious pig.

FADE OUT.

The barge didn't come and the food began to run out. More people were eating peanut butter and jam than ever before. They began to consider that the barge might not come for quite a while. They had finished planting all the trees the day before. How long had they been on this island? At least a month. Perhaps two.

Veronica's leg became infected. Every morning Betty asked Karl if the barge would come. Every morning he said he had no idea. Betty went back to the tent she shared with Veronica and told her maybe. They had run out of denial supplies, no more pot, no more acid. Reality was the weirdest drug. Veronica often screamed at night from the pain in her leg. She attacked the flies that tried to land on her. She captured them in her hand and squeezed. She became good at capturing flies. There was no longer anything else to do.

Una began to ration food. Isaak stopped trying to film her. Neil spoke to no one. His lips were often blue. Boredom and fear filled their waking hours. The Africans swam, the French dug holes.

The Africans and the French refused to speak English. This made communication impossible, but there was very little to say. Natasha cried often and Isaak comforted her with, "The barge will come tomorrow, you'll see." There was no more fuel for the crummy so no one went to the well to get water. They had been drinking out of the lake for days, although Una tried to keep it a secret. There were fewer and fewer secrets between them.

One night Una and Isaak were in her tent. The lake water was now only a foot away from Isaak's tent and he had become afraid to sleep there. He hadn't considered moving it because the barge would be coming the next day. It must. If not, then the day after. As long as there were no storms the shoreline could hold a few more days, but Isaak also slept with Una because their islands were eroding as well and they used each other as barricades.

Natasha broke down under the weight of Caesar and went to live in Little Africa. She refused to speak English as well, only her native Russian, which not even Caesar understood. All he wanted was the whiteness of her skin and her blue lips around his blackness.

The cook and Isaak together. He took her shirt off as if he had just invented the gesture. They must pretend. The condoms were all used up so they soaked in their own juices into the nights, uncaring of consequence. Isaak no longer needed the barge, he was being transported away through her. She stopped cooking for them. "Help yourselves," she said. Then at night their new ritual, like they invented it. Desperate pleasures. Interrogating moments. Finding tattoos. Isaak asked if she wanted to dance.

She and Isaak together on the sand. Another she. They held each other, breathing hard. Moses' portal loomed large a few metres away on the beach. Their feet shuffled in the sand in no particular pattern. The moon would be romantic under different circumstances. The logs in the lake were clunking softly, testing their boundaries.

Isaak threw the handi-cam into the lake. He felt liberated from Uzma's eyes.

A bear showed up in camp. Isaak was asleep in Una's tent when it happened. The bear ripped open his tent in his absence, simply wanting his bag of garbage, the fruit rinds. Isaak discovered it later and told Simon, because Simon was still acting as if he was in charge. Of course Isaak could have told anyone and the news would be everywhere in minutes. Simon got the gun. Isaak tried to have Karl stop him but all hierarchies had finally broken down. Everyone had become an individual island, living only for the barge, fighting over the remains of the peanut butter. They scraped jars daily. Simon took the gun and headed into the forest to hunt down the bear.

Simon was in the forest, had never used a gun before, his head ballooning from acid flashbacks. The lack of food and the mercury-laced water had provided their own high to Simon's susceptible brain. He was crawling on all fours looking for movement, the gun cradled in his arms, an army recruitment commercial. His mohawk was now a faded green, the brown roots grown out. He picked through the forest like a beast. He wanted bear.

He saw a movement through the trees and crawled a little closer. It was a large animal obstructed by branches. Simon twirled his lip ring unconsciously with his tongue. He aimed the rifle and pulled the trigger.

"Holy Fuck!" came the cry from the beast.

Suddenly Simon realized with horror that he had just shot Neil. No one will miss him, he thought. Best not to tell anyone. Simon moved closer. Neil lay in the moss, unconscious but breathing. There was a huge patch of blood around his stomach. As Simon watched, the entire shirt went red. Simon ran over his options: leave him here or bring him back to camp. Either way there was no hope for him. Simon took off his purple satin shirt and wrapped it around the wound. He only wore clothes from the Tickle Trunk now. Simon found Neil's tent a few metres away and dragged him into it. He brought the gun back to the kitchen and everyone's eyes were large.

"We heard a shot, did you get him?"

"Nothing out there, folks," said Simon. "The gun went off by accident."

Caesar accused Pierre of stealing a chocolate bar from his tent. A fight ensued. The Africans came running from their village, the French came out of the forest. They shoved each other, threw a few punches and insulted each other in many languages. They used the opportunity to vent. Natasha and Una screamed for them to stop and they did because they were too tired to resist any more. Natasha pulled Caesar off Pierre and took him back to Little Africa to tend to his wounds. No one was seriously hurt, some pride, some black eyes. The devout Muslim renounced the other Africans and retired to his tent to pray for deliverance.

When Piggy kept hanging around the kitchen quonset, whining pathetically, Isaak decided to search for Neil, in the hope that he could get her to stop. Isaak found Neil in his tent swimming in his own blood. The empty nitrous oxide cartridges were floating in pools made by the uneven ground. Perhaps he'd inhaled the last of them to ward off the pain of his final moments. It was a grotesque sight, his snub face now calm. The blackflies poured in when Isaak unzipped the tent. He quickly zipped it back up and proceeded to find Simon, who was fishing in the lake.

"There are no fish in that lake, Simon."

"I know."

"Then what are you doing?"

"Have to do something," he lisped back irritated.

"You shot Neil, didn't you?"

Simon had his shirtless back turned to him and Isaak examined the brands and tattoos there. There was a long pause while Simon stared at his fishing line which disappeared into the lake. The line plumbed between two logs.

"It was an accident."

"Jesus Christ, Simon. Why didn't you say something?"

"Nothing could be done for him." Simon started to cry. The brands on his back flared, these scars self-inflicted.

It was true. There was nothing to be done, nothing to be done but wait. Betty left, walking until she could get help for Veronica. Wandering the labyrinth of dirt roads searching for anything.

Isaak asked Una if she was as good a swimmer as a dancer.

"I can swim. Why?"

"I figure it's the only way out of here. We have to start admitting the facts."

"It would take a week, Isaak. It takes two days by barge."

"The barge isn't coming."

"Sure it is. Listen, I saved us some hummus. Hungry?"

"I am going to try and swim for it."

"Then good-bye, Isaak."

Isaak felt a certain victory in being the one to leave. The next morning he fueled up on hummus, greased himself with what was left of the butter and slipped away. He said good-bye to no one. She was still asleep when he went.

The water was frigid so his heart was forced to become a stone. Isaak swam to the middle of the lake where he felt another panic attack coming on. He held onto a floating log to calm himself. He used it for balance for some time, his arms wrapped around it like a trophy. He floated with the log in the direction he believed was south. The sun beat down. He climbed up onto the log but kept falling off because his balance had suffered. Eventually he just hung on and floated. Night. Day. The tortoises had passed on. There were new patterns on the mountains. No barge was to be seen. Night. Day.

Isaak went ashore to look for something to eat. He found some berries. He dried himself in the sun on the deserted beach. The flies drank from him. The monotonous waves created a rhythm like planting. Isaak knew he would never plant trees again. He stopped fearing deadheads. He had become numb.

Isaak began to forget the names for things. The space above him filled with rain.

Isaak became the beast of the lake.

The barge captain fished him out at high noon. Isaak was blistered by the sun and mumbling something about a propane torch. The captain was confused, but took him to his small quarters to lie down and gave him some food and water. Isaak was grateful. His vacant eyes looked off to the side of the captain's face as he asked questions.

Isaak told the barge captain about the camp and what had happened. He did not tell him everything.

"I assumed the contract was over and you guys flew out of there two weeks ago," the captain said.

Isaak lifted himself up to his full height as evidence that this was not so. His hair was matted, his face covered in grime, like the poster, his body unsure.

"Very well," said the captain in an agitated tone, "I guess I'll stop by there on my route. I have a very busy route, you know. It may not seem that way because the barge is so slow. There are plenty of others who need me."

Isaak gave himself over to the captain and focused his eyes on the clearcuts evident in the distance.

A Seven Letter Word

The young boy often went to the restaurant to sit at the player piano. Over the tinkle of cutlery the piano would spin its roll and bellows would push the peddles. The boy sat on the bench unnoticed. The management let him stay because he never did anything except sit at the piano. Eventually the boy, as many boys are apt to do, began to mimic. His hands followed the keys as they played. His small fingers could not reach an octave but he kept practicing. He never told anyone in his family about his visits to the restaurant. His mother would have scolded him for being in such a place, where men and women push pepper shakers across tables to each other, talk of romance, argue over the bill, drink too hard.

The young boy's mother was Anglican. She often read the lesson on Sunday. She sometimes filled in for the church organist but she was inexperienced and could only play a couple of hymns. When the organist was taken ill, the congregation knew instinctively which hymns to sing. His father was a hard worker, used his muscles every day. He had a moving truck with which he earned his living. The family lived in a third storey apartment on the edge of the city. In the summers the boy would ride in his father's truck and help with the smaller furniture, the lamps, some books.

One such summer the boy came home from the restaurant where he had been learning the latest roll on the player piano. A new one came in every month. By now he had a repertoire of about six songs that he had learned to mimic exactly. His father and mother were talking excitedly about something. He never saw his father show such enthusiasm. He was still dressed in his work overalls.

"The lady said that since her husband died, and he was the only one to play it, she had no use for it. She told me to get rid of it."

"But how are you going to get it in here?"

"The window."

"But we're on the third floor."

His father let out a laugh and told his wife not to worry, that he knew some people and that it would be there tomorrow. The boy was excited. This was conversation he was not used to. He felt as if he had entered a new land where the customs had all changed. Because he was no longer certain what was expected of him, he silently went to his room.

The next day he awoke to the sound of machinery. He left his room and stared at the scene taking place in his parents' living room. The huge bay window was letting in the morning light. The glass had been taken out. His mother stood with her hands folded gently, smiling. His father was yelling instructions out the window.

At first the boy thought it was a huge kite. That perhaps he had not fully woken up and that this was still a dream. As it came closer, framed by the window, he could see that it was a piano. It hovered in the air outside the apartment, the morning's anomaly. His father grabbed one of the piano legs and steadied it. It was then that the boy noticed the rope suspending the piano from the roof. His father guided it into the room like a magician revealing a secret.

The rope slipped slightly and the piano fell the final few inches to the floor. The boy thought the sound it made was like thunder. The note filled the room in the same way the light coming through the window filled the room. The family stood waiting for the echo to subside.

"It's wonderful," the boy heard his mother say and she flung her arms around her husband. The boy had never seen his parents embrace before. The summer air came in the open window, filling the apartment with the smells from the bakery three stories below.

The boy wiped the sleep from his eyes and moved toward the new addition. It occupied the room like an idol. He stood over the keys. Standing, he was just the right height. He placed his small fingers on the ivory keys. His parents watched in amusement, pleased that their son was taking an interest. Perhaps he would like to learn. His mother could teach him the hymns she knew.

The boy opened with the popular rag of the day. He played effortlessly and flawlessly. His left hand bounced like a robin on a freshly cut lawn. The room was filled with music. In the street below the people who had lined up to buy bread that morning listened intently. The boy began to sweat. The man and woman watched their son with astonishment as their arms left the moment of their embrace.

*

She heard the music while waiting in line. She recognized it right away. Last night at the restaurant with Elias. The wine. The player piano was in the corner. They had had a table next to the kitchen. Waiters passed by every few minutes. It was that kind of restaurant.

She had been standing in line for her bread, waiting, for ten minutes now. It became this way after the last political crisis. Waiting for bread, waiting for everything. The music hit her as serendipity. It floated out of a third storey apartment above her head like memory, creeping into her.

There had been a yellow daisy in the middle of the table. The restaurant had supplied it. A waiter had come by their table, before they had even ordered the wine, carrying a bouquet of yellow daisies. He was placing them on all the tables at which couples were seated. The player piano spun and clicked, filling the restaurant with music. At first she thought the young boy was playing but realised his feet couldn't touch the peddles yet; they were moving under their own power. She thought the boy was slightly odd, following along. She had noticed the daisy was put in a glass with no water. She felt dry and asked for the wine list to hide her discomfort. She wanted a sweet wine but Elias preferred the dry.

She was almost at the counter. The woman in front of her was starting to make noises that seemed to have a weight of impatience. Only pieces of her monologue could be made out over her chronic mumble. At the counter the woman in front of her barked out her order for sixteen loaves of eggbread.

"Sliced?" said the woman behind the counter.

The woman in front of her threw up her hands and screamed in a language that was unfamiliar to all of them. The crowd of women stood silently like lakes after a rain, ready to overflow.

Elias Huffman had commented on the daisy. On the colour. She appreciated this trait in him but was rendered incapacitated by her fear of being misinterpreted, so she said nothing. This allowed him to talk about himself, which is what he wanted to do anyway. It turned out that he was a writer. He told her about the feeling he got while running long distances. It was a drug, he had said. He said everyone is addicted to something. If you're not then you're addicted to hope. He told her about freshly cut lawns, about a failed savings and loan manager who had decided to become a photographer after recovering from a car crash. He told her about the track. He told her.

She asked for her eggbread. Only two loaves. "It's just for myself," she heard herself saying and then feeling uncomfortable. In the bakery, the music was muffled by the noisy women. She wanted to listen to the music coming from the sky. She wished it were night so that the streets would offer her more anonymity. She craved anonymity and the defences it afforded. She paid for her loaves of bread and left the women. On the street she was comforted by the sound of the music and began her journey home.

Although Elias Huffman was anosmiatic, and knew he would be unable to detect its scent, he sniffed the daisy out of propriety. She seemed impressed when he did this and in what, to him, was an outward act of boldness, she demanded to see a wine list. The boy sitting at the piano was distracting him. The name of this rag had something to do with a bird, but he was unsure how to approach this woman and ask her if she recognised it. It was the song he had once danced to with his wife, in the kitchen one morning, while the coffee was being made. The coffee had been bitter and had come from a country he had never heard of. It was his wife who had spoken the name of the bird. A thrush, a starling, a crow. A song about a crow? This was before the separation. It was snowing outside but nothing was sticking.

He told her he was a writer, although he had never written anything other than a letter. He told her about the next letter he was going to write as if it were a novel. Although he mentioned the story about the freshly cut lawn when he was nine, and the bee which he had stepped on, he never told her about his wife. No one else seemed to notice the boy. It was the music that made him believe he was there now. The boy at the piano was only a prop for his memory.

The music filled the restaurant mingling with the smoke. From under the window draughts of air were exposed like fingerprints in the smoky room. The couples filled corners, sharing wine, sometimes a Cosmopolitan. He knew little about wine. He knew only that he liked it dry. Because she was so bold in ordering, he felt it would only be right if she had her way with the sweet. The boy was concentrating hard. Like running, he thought. He's running with his fingers. He remembered himself as a boy. On the freshly cut grass, before the bee had stung him.

His parents were in lawn chairs listening to the radio, drinking and arguing about money. He had been practicing his running. From the tree at the back of the yard to the window of the house. And back again. Then the bee sting. It was a bad sting and Mr. and Mrs. Huffman considered the fact that he might be allergic, because he had never been stung before. They were cautious parents. They took him to the hospital where he remained for three days. He did, in fact, swell to enormous proportions. His parents visited him separately. They would express enormous concern as he languished in their attention. After three days he was released from the hospital and his father was no longer living in the house with his mother. He blamed himself and the bee. His guilt was like poison inside of him.

The boy at the piano was unaware of how the others in the restaurant perceived him. He didn't care. He was willing to leave if the owner asked, but the owner never asked.

She ordered pasta, he meat.

Back at her apartment Elias asked if he should remove his shoes. She told him that he should not. He had already untied the laces, but now he retied them extra tight so that it felt numb in his small toe.

She asked him if he wanted a drink and of course he did. She brought out more wine and some eggbread.

"I know nothing at all about wines," he confessed.

"Me neither."

"But at the restaurant. You seemed to know what you wanted."

"I don't usually do that. I don't usually know."

She passed Elias a wine glass and he took it and drank half of the glass before he thanked her.

"Sweet," he said.

"Yes," she said.

He put his glass on the kitchen counter and leaned in to kiss her. She pulled away. He picked up his glass, took another sip of wine, and then moved closer to her. Nervously she turned her back and opened the ice box.

"Ice?" she asked with her back turned to him.

"In wine?"

"Oh. Of course not. Sorry."

Elias's finger touched the back of her thigh where her skirt met her leg. She spun around, her skirt billowing, and asked him to leave.

"Is that why you never let them take off their shoes?"

"Just leave. Please. I think you..."

Elias Huffman sat down at the kitchen table and began to read the newspaper.

"They arrested two more today. It's terrible."

"Yes," she said with uncertainty, "it certainly is."

He read the newspaper cover to cover. The kitchen was silent except for the hum of the overhead light and her repetition of the word *Please* under her breath. She was unsure of what he was capable. She measured time with the turn of the pages, the flap of paper in the pregnant room.

At one point he stopped and raised his finger at her. She stood beside the ice box, still frozen. He touched the side of his head with his finger as if remembering something. Without looking at her he said, "A robin. It was about a robin." He resumed reading.

After Elias had finished the paper, he said goodbye, and walked out. When the door was safely locked, she crossed the room to her radio, flicked it on, and sat in the chair to cry. The newspaper lay open to the crossword puzzle. One across was a seven letter word for a musical genius. The radio was playing the latest rag. The music filled her kitchen unconditionally.

That night the boy slept soundly, unaware of the miracle to come the next morning from out of the sky.

Acknowledgements

For their support I would primarily like to thank my parents.

These stories were written and revised over a long period of time and many people offered feedback and encouragement along the way. I'd like to thank: Ouma Seeks Ouzo, Liane Keightley, Peter Paré, Ummni Khan, Carrin Christie, Dana Bath, Corey Frost, Catherine Kidd, Anne Stone, Billy Mavreas, my sister and cousins, Taien Ng-Chan, Colin Christie, Marc Bell, Lance Blomgren, A Week in the Woods, St. Remy, rob mclennan, Terry Lister, Charles Austin, Rob Lutes, Matthew Firth, Mark Clay, and Michael Turner.

Thanks to Rob Allen and Steve Luxton for their editorial feedback and commitment to the maintenance of literary activity in Montreal.

And, of course, thanks to Meg Sircom for everything.

"Sleeves Sewn Shut": Published as a single story chapbook by conundrum press, 1996. Honourable Mention in QWF/CBC Award 2001 and subsequently printed in *Telling Stories: New English Writing from Quebec* (Véhicule Press), 2002

"A Seven Letter Word": *Agent*, 1996

"The Sacrifice": *Border/Lines* #44, 1997

"Bakhtin on Sabbatical": *Border/Lines* #44, 1997

"Writers Get Real Jobs" was originally a limited edition chapbook by conundrum press called *Booked into the Wartime: Literary Figures Adopt New Careers,* 1997

"Shopping for Contacts": *Moosemilk: Best of the Moosehead Anthology* (DC Books), 1999

"Missing the Whippet": *Helios*, 1999

"How to Build a Wall in 12 Easy Steps": Originally published as a conundrum press chapbook, 1999. Reprinted in *You & Your Bright Ideas: New Montreal Writing* (Véhicule Press), 2001

"Looking for Parking": *Headlight Anthology* #3, 2000

"4 1/2 on the Main": *Blood & Aphorisms* #37, 2000

"Doing Time": An excerpt entitled "At the Metro" appeared in *Blood & Aphorisms* #37, 2000

"Caleb's Auto": Published as *Caleb*, a single-story chapbook by conundrum press Distroboto imprint with drawings by Marc Bell, 2003

Andy Brown is the co-editor of *You & Your Bright Ideas: New Montreal Writing* (Véhicule Press) and *Running with Scissors* (Cumulus Press). He is a contributing editor for *Matrix* magazine and the founder of conundrum press.